JESSIE KESSON

was born Jessie Grant McDonald in Inverness in 1915, and soon moved to Elgin with her beloved mother (she never knew her father). Estranged from many of the family, mother and daughter were forced to live off their own resources, and Jessie's early days were spent dodging the Cruelty Inspector and the rent man, before she was sent to an orphanage in Skene, Aberdeenshire. As a teenager, she entered service, settling in 1934 on a farm with her husband Johnnie, a cottar. Those early years have inspired much of her work: the novels, *The White Bird Passes* (1958), *Glitter of Mica* (1963) and *Another Time, Another Place* (1983), as well as short stories such as *Where the Apple Ripens* (1985). *The White Bird Passes* and *Another Time, Another Place* were prize-winning films in 1980 and 1983 respectively. All of Jessie Kesson's books are published by Virago.

Until recently, whether she was writing stories, poems, newspaper features, dramas or novels, Jessie Kesson has always done other jobs. She has been a cinema cleaner, an artists' model and was, for nearly twenty years, a social worker in London and Glasgow. Now a great-grandmother, and the proud owner of a 'scarlet goon' (conferred by Dundee University in 1984), she lives with Johnnie in London, where she is currently writing the story of her remarkable life and a dramatisation of *Glitter of Mica*.

Jessie Kesson

GLITTER
OF
MICA

Published by VIRAGO PRESS Limited 1993
20–23 Mandela Street, Camden Town, London NW1 0HQ

First published in Great Britain by Chatto & Windus Ltd 1963
Copyright © Jessie Kesson 1963
Virago edition offset from The Hogarth Press 1963 edition

A CIP catalogue record for this book is available from the British Library

Printed in Great Britain by Cox & Wyman Ltd., Reading, Berks.

FOR
ELIZABETH ADAIR

This is the shape of a land which outlasts a strategy
And is not to be taken by rhetoric or arms.

G. S. FRASER *Hometown Elegy*

THE parish of Caldwell lies to the east of our shire. It has moved neither poet to song nor tourist to praise. It has little to give or lend but much to sell; Ayrshire and Friesian cattle pastured out for milk, Aberdeen Angus cattle reared for fattening, for this is cattle and barley country, and both, and second to none, are flaunted in the face of the world.

On Soutar Hill, to the north of Caldwell, you can, on a fine clear day, see the figure of a horse carved out in stone from Pictish times, and whatever the weather and from any direction you can see the old Free Kirk, one of the first of the kirks to break away from the Old Established Church, in the Disruption of 1843. Although it stands as intact now as it stood then, the Free Kirk has become a granary, for the people of Caldwell are less kirk conscious than were their forbears. The Misses Lennox, retired from Town, bought the Free Kirk Manse and the wood surrounding it, renaming the latter "Lob's Wood", but to those who were born and bred in Caldwell, it stubbornly remains "The Free Kirk Wood".

Caldwell is surrounded by old "Houses" occupied by old names: Forbes-Sempill. Seaton. Hamilton. And by castles whose owners are of Norman origin: Farquharson. Gordon. Grant. Duff. So, considering its proximity to ancient aristocracy, the wonder is that Caldwell has neither legends of its own, nor the ballads which arise from them. It is content to borrow these from its neighbours, so it laughs in recollection of the Laird of Udny's Fool, reminiscing satirically . . . "I'm the Laird of Udny's Fool. Whose Fool are *you*?" . . . Weeps in its cups over Fyvie's *Bonnie Peggie*, or goes singing in its stride with *The Irish Dragoon* who died for love of her.

Early in the morn they set out for Aberdeen.
Early in the morning O!
And when they marched across the bonnie brig o' Gight
The band it played "The Lowlands o' Fyvie", O!

Long long before they reached Old Meldrum Town
They had their Captain to carry O!
Long long before they reached bonnie Aberdeen
They had their Captain to bury O!

And drunk or sober it becomes bawdy over *The White Cow of Turriff*.

Caldwell also borrows the neighbouring gentry to declare open its Summer Fetes and Shows. A token gesture this, to those who feel that they "have come down in the World", and an incentive to those who still hope to "get on in the World", though, to most of its inhabitants, Caldwell *is* "The World".

Last summer it was Lady Grizelda Beaton who was "honoured and privileged" – or so she herself

8

maintained at the time – to declare open Caldwell's Summer Show. Indeed, Lady Grizelda got so carried away on the platform, that a few close observers, with no sense of occasion, gravely doubted whether Charlie Anson's carpentry, makeshift at the best of times, would hold its own anent all the prancing and gesticulating that was over her Ladyship. And when she stretched out her arms as if to embrace the whole wide world, vowing to Caldwell's inhabitants, gooking below, that they were "indeed her ain folk", whose who lived on their avowal of "Better Days" were deeply moved, although the same declaration had been examined closely and suspected strongly by God Knows and his fellow farm-workers; for Caldwell is first and foremost the land of the farm-worker.

"It's our vote yon one's smarming after," had been God Knows' considered opinion, but then, he belonged to a race which not only suspected everybody outwith the farm he worked on, but most of those within it too. "For yon second son of hers is just down from Oxford," he had recollected, "and going in for politics. Or so they say."

"But it's No Ball. And Up the Liberals!" Dod Feary had shouted in his cups, which slogan had visibly cooled down the remainder of Lady Grizelda's speech, for had her claim that they "were indeed her ain folk" been true, she would have known this much about them at least, that the odds were always on the farm-worker's vote going to his farmer's Party, just as in older times when his forbears with native sagacity had attended the Kirk of their farmer's religious persuasion.

This was a conditioning which had come down through the centuries and was automatic and, in its way, a kind of comfort. For the farmer was their "Fatherhood", good or bad, and the farm-workers took the fierce privilege of sons in passing judgment on this issue, either way he was their own, so rooted that he became identified with the land itself, his name absorbed into the very title of the acres he farmed. Even the old hereditary aristocrats of the countryside needed a double identification; Forbes of Rothiemay, one said. Hay of Seaton. Gordon of Huntly. Grant of Monymusk. Cowdray of Dunecht. But the farmers had need of no such prefixes to become landmarks, for though they died at last, their earth abideth and their identification with it was simplified and perpetuated by the syllabic titles of their farms: Auchronie. Ardgye. Balblair. Balben. Calcots. Clova. Drumdelgie. Delgaty and . . . Darklands.

*   *   *

Darklands is one of Caldwell's largest farms, its productivity high, its soil fertile, its landscape bleak. The kind of place will cause a Townsman in passing to thank God for the fury of his factory or the fuss of his fishmarket, but to the men who work on Dark-

lands farm, even the two or three isolated landmarks on its landscape become unnecessary at last.
Occasionally, they will lift their eyes towards Soutar
Hill to verify that the Pictish horse still stands in
stone – always aware that it could rear nowhere else.
Whiles, too, they will straighten their backs and
gaze on their other landmark, Ambroggan House,
for it isn't every parish that provides asylum for the
wealthy mentally ill of the land. It was the Plunger
who long ago had puzzled it all out for his fellow
farm-workers:

"Just you take Chae Finnie. Him that was Handy-
man over there at Balwhine. And yon night that he
up and chased the Vet in his shirt tail with a scythe
in his hand. Clean mad Chae had gone, we all said.
And until the Authorities came and carted him off
to the Asylum, not a man, woman, chick or child of
us opened our mouths to Chae for fear of the madness that had come over him, for all that we had
known him all our days with him as sane as ourselves. But yet, mark you! We pass the time of day
with the patients from Ambroggan House, and them
with us. As happy as if we were all in our right minds.
You see, it's all just a question of money again. If
you're poor you're plain mad. If you're rich they've
got an easier name for you. A Nervous breakdown.
And yet, the odd thing about it is we *were* all far more
scared of poor Chae Finnie than ever we are when
we run into the Daft Dominie from Ambroggan

House, just speaking away to himself by the side of the road. It would near look as though money mellows the degree of madness itself. Or maybe it's just that our respect for money makes a rich madman less fearful than a poor madman!"

Hugh Riddel, Head Dairyman at Darklands, stood remembering that now. Minding, too, how he had thought at the time that there maybe was something in what the Plunger had said, though he had laughed it off, and had ordered the Plunger to stop speaking stuff and nonsense, and to keep on plunging the milk bottles in the tank.

Hugh Riddel tried to keep his eyes averted from the wooded outline of Ambroggan House, for when time and tide stood still, place itself could petrify you within it, allowing you to escape into the future, and always less than you were. But even had he foreseen that, Hugh Riddel realised, he could not – nor would not – have averted it. Strange how a man, a man like Hugh Riddel, could have compelled himself forward so far and fast, till at last he had lost his bearings, and could only grope his way back through a bleak known-ness.

This surely was the bleakest landscape in Scotland. Morayshire now. Ah! But there was a mellow country for you. Hot to the sun and comforted by trees. A lass of a land and comely. Hugh Riddel's memories of Morayshire were brief, but safe and warm in recollection. Then his people had moved south to work on a farm near Stonehaven. Bleak land there too, with the sea biting always at hand. Still, it was on that farm near Stonehaven that he had grown old enough to realise that all the comings and goings to work on different farms were not for his parents the fine adventures they had been for himself.

A farm-worker was fee'd to work on a farm for a year only. At the end of the year the farmer would either "seek" him to "bide on for another year", or remain ominously silent on the subject. If his silence remained unbroken when lambing-time came round, the farm-worker knew that his services were no longer required. The sack without words. Hugh Riddel could marvel over the simplicity of it still. And the re-engaging of a farm-worker was equally simple. No written contract; just the passing of "Arles" – a sun ranging from half a crown to ten shillings – by the farmer to his prospective worker, to seal and "wet the bargain". Hugh Riddel could marvel over the simplicity of that too.

His father had seldom been asked to "bide on" at any farm when his year was up. It was always his mother who took this so much to heart. He could see her now, shrunken by memory, a small body forever wringing her hands, so that she fluttered tiny and distressed in his mind. He could see himself too, a small boy speeding perpetually through spring mirks, always the apprehensive – but excited – bearer of the bad tidings.

"The First Horseman's just been asked to bide on.
I heard the farmer seeking him in the stable!"

His father banging his fist on the table and shaking
the silence in the kitchen.

"What of it, then? Good God, it's but early yet.
We're only into Februar'. The farmer's got till
March to seek me to bide on."

"But you are the *Cattleman*, Father." He heard his
ten-year-old self insist. "You are the Cattleman. And
the Cattleman is always asked to bide on before the
First Horseman."

Hugh Riddel knew now exactly what his wife Isa
meant, when she accused him of not only "Baking
the cake" but "Icing it as well. And putting on all
the decorations, so that there is nothing left for
anybody else to do at all, except to admire it and
eat it."

Even at the age of ten he had allowed no loop-
holes, and could remember how his father had
always struggled to find one.

"What of it, then? There are *other* farms in Scotland. And I have never yet been feared of bending
my back. There are other farms I tell you!"

"Aye. And we've tried a gey few of them," had
always been his mother's brief and bitter response.

"What of it?" His father had demanded again.
"We haven't been happy here. Not a one of us. It's
too near the sea for one thing. And we are inland
folk for another thing. Not seafarers. God Almighty,

woman. Even Robbie Burns' father couldna thole
this part of the country. That's why he upped it and
made for away down the South, yonder!"

The smile broke into Hugh Riddel's thoughts. His
father had always tried to translate his failings into
strengths, through comparison with Burns. A comparison which never moved his mother, for Burns, as
she often said, "just never won round her at all".
Come to think of it, though, for all Burns' reputed
success with "The Lasses" of his day, it was the
women of the countryside who now remained more
immune to his "Memory". "The men", as his mother
so often remarked, "just uses Burns as an excuse for
theirselves!" And that had been another of the times
when the excuse hadn't worked with his mother.

"I don't give a tinker's curse for *what* Robbie
Burns' father thought of this part of the country," she
had protested. "He's no concern of mine at all. All
I'm concerned with is that you have lost this job too.
Just as you've lost every job you've ever had. I'm
sick and tired of it all. And of you and your light
fingers! We are no better off than the tinkers. We
are always on the top of the road."

"Do you imagine, woman," his father had flared,
"Do you imagine for one minute that I am the only
man on this farm that helps myself to a pucklie oats
for my hens? It's just that I always happen to get
found out."

*   *   *

Oh, and then the spring would grope forward towards the Term, and into the month of May with its small Feeing Market Days. It was then you could see the farm-workers who hadn't been asked to bide on mount their bicycles and go slanting down the roads that led to the little Market towns, whistling with all the defiance in the world, syne standing clustered round the Market Cross, trying to look as likely lads as possible, while waiting for the farmers to size them up and approach them with the offer of another year's Fee.

"Just like a curran Clydesdale horse taking round the ring," as God Knows had once recalled it. Except that the brute beasts had their natural dignity. For they never kenned that they were being sized up. And they wouldn't have cared a docken if they had kent.

It was then, too, that you could see the farm-workers who had been asked to bide on, planting out their "yards" – never "gardens" – with the bare essentials, curly kale and first early potatoes. There was never enough security to plant anything as frivolous but enduring as a lilac bush. Hugh Riddel's mother had always had an awful hankering after a lilac bush, yet never enough faith to plant one. "Not for *other* folk to get the good of," as she often explained. For that was another deeply ingrained aversion. The fear of other folk getting the good of anything outwith their own efforts. It wasn't until they had come to Darklands, here, that his mother began to take any interest in the yard, and started to call it by the name of garden.

*   *   *

Hugh Riddel could remember as clear as anything the night on which his father had come home from the market, fee'd to Darklands. 1939. The year the war broke out.

"*Well* now! Who was it said I would never get another fee to another farm?" his father had demanded, jocularly, but with fierce under-currents of pride. "Who was it, then? For you can just swallow your words, and take a right good look at this for a start-off!"

"This" was a ten-shilling note that his father had wagged under their noses. And his mother and himself *had* taken a good look. For money – paper money, that was – was something they only set eyes on twice a year, on Term Days.

"Well may you both stand there gooking," his father had said, pleased with the wordless spell the ten-shilling note had cast over them. "And that's only the Arles that Darklands gave me to wet the bargain. Truth tells twice, you see!" he had added with the wonderful simplicity of one who had just found that out.

"It's a wonder to me you didn't go and drink the lot," his mother said, when she recovered herself.

But there had been no barb in her voice, and they both knew by the way she fussed around getting the supper that she was pleased too.

"But I had a drink," his father expanded, conscious of the geniality in the air. "For I had something to drink to. You'll both grant that, when you hear what else I've got to tell you. This is my Fee now." . . . Even his mother, who so seldom stood still, stopped fiddling about with supper to listen, while his father counted everything off on his fingers.

"Meal. Six bolls of it. Tatties. Ten bags. Not counting two bags of First Earlies. Coal. A ton. And another half-ton extra for calving times. Now, Mother, just you consider that extra half-ton itself! There's not many farmers take into account the coal we burn up night after night sitting up waiting for the cows to calve. So *that's* not to be sneezed at. Syne there's two quarts of milk a day. All the skimmed milk you care to carry home. And of course the first milk after calving is mine, so we'll have plenty of calfie's cheese. And you're both gey fond of calfie's cheese. That, then, that's our perquisites for the year. Now for my Fee. Oh, but you'll never guess my Fee, Hugh, son. Never in a month of Sundays. So I may just as well tell you what it is. Seventy-six pounds a year. Seventy-six pounds. The biggest Fee I've ever been offered. What do you think of it, then? Well? Have the pair of you gone and lost the use of your tongues?"

Hugh Riddel couldn't remember his own Fee

exactly. It had gone up by leaps and bounds. Somewhere in the region of seven hundred it would be.
Strange that it was his father's Fee of twenty years
ago which lit his memory with golden numerals. Six
feet high. Seventy-six pounds a year.

What a perfect night that had been while it lasted.
For nothing lasted long, least of all – perfection.

"And there's another thing!" His father had remembered. "And it will please you as well. I'll never
again lay unlawful hands on an ear of corn. Darklands herd is T.T. Tested, so we're not allowed to
keep hens."

"What? No *hens*?" His mother had protested dis-
mayed. "But I've always had my two three hens.
Always."

"I can make neither head nor tail of you, woman,"
his father had puzzled. "You were always complain-
ing that your hens died in debt. Look see! I'll tell you
what. We'll sell the lot. Bantams and all. And we'll
buy a bit of new linoleum with the price of them. For
you've been making a sore enough cry for new linoleum. How's that, my quean? Come on, now. Come
in about to me till I tell you something else!"

"Get away with you, man. You're drunk!" had
been his mother's invariable reply to such overtures
from his father; and her reaction to scurry away out
into the scullery, beyond reach of husband or plea
of son.

"I'm far from drunk, woman," his father would

protest to her disappearing figure, turning to confide in the small boy he had been. "What would you make of that, Hugh, son? Your mother says I'm drunk. I come home to her with a bonnie Fee to a bonnie farm, and your mother shows no pleasure. Though she would be the first to make fine lament if I'd come home without a Fee at all. I try to say a bonnie wordie to her, and she turns and tells me that I'm drunk."

"The only time your father ever does say a bonnie wordie to me," his mother's voice came from the scullery in defence, "is when he is drunk."

It was true, too, Hugh Riddel remembered, but only as a *kind* of truth. For his father's words of endearment had always been spare and difficult, needing high moments for utterance, and his reaction to rejection, blustering but helpless.

"Now, now, my quean. That's just enough of that. Come here now. Come on in about to me. God, but there's just a handful of you. And I could lift you clean above my head with one hand, if I'd a mind to."

He could, too. Hugh Riddel remembered that as well, although he had seldom seen it happen. He remembered it because it had feared him. His father spanning his mother's waist with his two hands and lifting her clean over his shoulder in a whirl of petticoats and skirling. It had feared him as much as if they had been in anger with each other, but it had strangely excited him, too.

"My God," he had thought. "When *I* am big!" With no other words to expand the thought, or define and clarify it. Only small wordless images and sensations, like his memories of Morayshire; the coarse comforting smell of sharn, the bare fire-scorched legs of the farmhouse servant girls, their laughter, and the dark skirls of them coming from the hay lofts. Himself high up on the turnip-sowing machine, the turnip seeds running between his fingers. He had always felt very safe, seated on the sowing machine, playing in the darkness with the turnip seeds, yet always apprehensive, as though he were on the brink of something still unknown, but which he would one day discover, and feel as much at one with as he felt with the tiny dark seeds that trickled through his fingers.

He was always greatly relieved – and just as greatly surprised – that at such times his parents hadn't simply lifted the lid clean off all his private thoughts, and stood staring at them, shocked and angry. They never did, of course. He was so often simply a means of communication between them; particularly with his mother. He could hear her yet.

"Ah well, Hugh. Darklands, or no Darklands, Fine Fee or no Fee at all, we are for the top of the road again, as usual. That will mean some other new school for you again. My! But you should be a clever man yet, with all the different schools you've attended in your time."

"But I like new schools fine," he had mumbled. Partly out of complete truth, and partly from a desire to side with his father. "And maybe, maybe, Father, there will be tractors at Darklands farm."

"Maybe there will be at that, then." His father had grasped the lifeline. "That wouldn't surprise me one bit. Mind you, Hugh, tractors are fine enough for clay soil and rough going, but for a bit of company in a long day, give me a pair of horse. God, Hugh. Did ever I get round to telling you about a Horseman I once kent? He always insisted on sleeping out in the stable with his pair. I wight he did that! For he always vowed that he preferred the brutes' company to that of the chield he was bothied with. A terrible man it appeared for snoring and wetting his bed. Though, come to think of it now, I believe I'd prefer the company of a pair of horse to a man like that, myself!"

And, as always, it was his mother who disrupted such moments with the flick of her tongue:

"Good grief, man. Have you nothing better to do but sit there and stuff Hugh's head with a lot of dirt!"

But nothing quite diminished the glow that their minds had cast over Darklands, the new farm that they were going to work on. Even now Hugh Riddel recollected their anticipation, as through some bright upstanding springtime. Darklands, they had gathered from the farm-workers' grapevine, was a Farm of Farms.

"Not a single pair of horse on yon place," the Second Cattleman had informed them. "It's all tractor work there now. And Darklands himself is a gentleman farmer at that. Oh, but you'll have a good enough sit down with him, Riddel. For there's no side to yon man at all. And devil the chance of *him* ever trying to catch you out, by creeping up behind you on a mirky morning, looking like one of ourselves."

If Hugh Riddel had ever been asked to define comfort, he would have described it as standing young in that spring, under the cover of old men's voices, his face towards the sea, and half his mind on the mysterious life of the trawlers, drifting westwards to the Bay of Nigg. His remembrance on the strange turns of their speech, and lingering on the high whine of the fisherwives' voices.

... *I cast my net in Largo Bay. And fishes I caught nine.* ...

And drawing his cold face into the warm stable again, lending his ears to accents that were familiar, and to arguments that never varied in context.

"They say that Darklands doesn't hold with the Farm-workers' Union, though."

"Name me the farmer who does, Duggie."

"I'll go one better than that. I'll say again as I've said before, if every farm-worker upped and joined his Union, we'd have one of the strongest Unions in Scotland."

"All right, Duggie. All right. We know all about that, so don't you get going on Unions again, or we'll be here for the rest of the night! All *I'm* trying to do is to put old Riddel here wise to the bee in Darkland's bonnet. And that's not the Union, though I've heard tell he's not too struck on it. It's the cream off the top of his milk. *That's* what you've got to guard against, Riddel! For he'll come down on you like the hammers of hell if he catches you interfering with his cream. They tell me he never grudges a bit of firewood lifted from the steading on a dark night. And whiles, they say, he'll even turn a blind eye to the paraffin dwindling in the drum. But if you're ever found helping yourself to the cream off the top of his dairy cans, it's just God help you, and down the road with you. No explanations given. And none sought – if you're wise. For, you see, Darklands reasons that the customers who buy his milk are entitled to all the cream that rises on top of it."

"And sound enough reasoning at that! It's coming as I am aye trying to tell you all. It's coming on both sides. And it would all come a damned sight sooner if you just had the horse sense to join your Union."

"You and your Union again, Duggie. Bloody fine do you ken that it isn't so easy for a Union man to get a Fee."

"Fine do I ken that, Charlie. So for God's sake keep your hair on! The two three you've got left. All

I'm *trying* to say is this, if we were *all* Union men the farmers would have to Fee us. They'd have no option. For I'll grant you that they could put the army in to lift the tatties, aye, or to hoe the turnips at a stretch, but could you imagine Colonel McCombie yonder calving a cow?"

"Whiles, Duggie, whiles you do make me wonder. For you speak an awful lot of dirt! We're tied hand and foot. We always will be as long as our houses are part of our wage. Lose your job and you lose your house."

"Maybe. Maybe so. But it's coming. That I'm sure of. You and me may not live to see that day, Riddel. And Charlie there will certainly never see it, for if the drink doesn't kill him, the women will! But our sons might just see it. Your Hugh there, maybe he'll live long enough to see it, and benefit from it, when it comes."

*   *   *

And Hugh Riddel *had* seen it come. It came with the war. A revolution as complete as the Industrial Revolution, but quieter – and bloodless. If Hugh Riddel's father had still been alive he would not have recognised the farm of Darklands now. For, though it had been a farm of farms in his day, it was now a Model farm, bathrooms and electricity in all the cottar houses. A day off a week, a week-end off a month. Farm-workers running their own cars. And

Superannuation. Not even the rabid Duggie of childhood memory could ever have visualised such a benefit as a farm-worker with the security of a pension.

For most of his working life Hugh Riddel's father had known but two days off in the year. The "Term Days", at the end of May and November.

Golden days though. Hugh Riddel could recall them still with an uprising of excitement. The unfamiliar smell of bacon filling the kitchen, his mother clucking around the range, warning and worrying in the same breath.

"Dip your bread in the fat, Hugh. But the bacon's for Father. He's for the Town."

And his father big with the good humour that was over him.

"My best suit. The blue, the day. Pressed beneath the mattress three nights hard running. And how's *that* for a crease in my trousers, Hugh? It would just cut your throat, wouldn't it not now? It's as sharp as that! My bonnet, Hugh. Jump to it, son. Not *that* bonnet, you gowk! My Sunday bonnet. For I'm for the Town."

Even now, such excited preparation seemed just as it should be to Hugh Riddel. For it was a wild town, a wanton town, that farm-workers set out for on Term Days, and wide-eyed on the watch for country men. Though blind, its nose could still have sniffed them out with sharn for sweat, and deaf, its ears could still have recognised their tackett-booted tread, and their laughter rising ribald in Dobb's Café, and Dobb's market too, where siren women lurked behind the stalls, big bosomed, blonde, and honey-mouthed, or so they seemed to farm-workers on Term Days, luring their hard-won penny Fees with tartan trinkets.

"Come on now, Jock. This pouch should hold your six months' siller. In your own tartan too. 'By Dand', and *up* the Gordons!"

And teasingly, with bits of fripperies, would confront the lumbering red-faced men, whose hands had seldom fumbled anything finer than flannelette.

"This pair should fit your best lass, Jock. Think of the fun you'll have fitting them on her. Come, buy – for love's sake!"

Dobb's market was all for love's sake. Post-cards showing How. Books telling When. "The Chemist" – Quack – doing business all day long with herbs and pills and special advice in after hours. But dark and dear. And not for country men, grinning but stubborn, rejecting such abortive practices.

"We'll risk it yet. For the pill was never made would empty Bogie Bell of what Tom the Ternland gave her, six months come Friday, at Boynlie Ball."

Free of Dobb's market. Swerving to Baltic Cross – traditionally their own, and freemen of the Town for this one day. And down by Baltic Cross, teeming but islanded alien townsfolk caught in hurried passing the warm dissenting talk of cattle.

27

"We're tackling Ayrshires up our way."

"Dangerous vratches. Far too fond of hooking, Ayrshires. They rip each others' flanks to bits."

"For safety, give me a Red Poll."

"*Never*, man. Great fat hornless lumps, the Red Polls. Granted they don't hook each other, for they've got damn all to hook with. But, by God, they make up for that by lashing out. For a quiet-natured cow, now, give me the Guernsey."

"Too delicate a brute for this part of the country. A Guernsey needs as muckle care as a thoroughbred horse. Fair-weather beasts, Guernseys. No, no. For a good all-round cow there's just nothing to touch the Shorthorn. They're tough beasts and their yield's aye consistent."

And in the more exclusive haunts, the farmers talked of this and that. Of subsidies and costs, and how they were rising all the time. And never once, not even in trust amongst each other, confessed to profit. But down at Baltic Cross, made bold by beer and strengthened by each other, their workers claimed the leases of their lands by right of deed, and tenanted them with new ideas.

"If I was in Clayacre's shoes, I'd sell at Whitsun. For yon land's souring. It's fair worn out."

"High time too that Lower Ardgye grew less grain. Yon's not mixed farming. It's just grain forever up in yon place!"

"He'd need to let such land lie fallow for a while."

The last bus home. The thought of it ettling in their minds, like chaff that itched against their skins on threshing days. And all eyes eyes cocked against the sky for a reprieve, or even extension. Then watches, turnip-faced, dragged out to check the stars; their minds would stray to that wild pub down by the docks, and linger there, where women were as bold as brass, offering you all they had for one and sixpence. Near forcing't on you. It was just such women's haste, and the price they put upon it, made it immoral in farm-workers' eyes. Since they preferred it given, just for the love of it. Or, for at most a dozen new-laid eggs, and that but hansel. And, though their thoughts might linger in such places, their feet invariably but unsteadily led them buswards, yet with a kind of virtue. "For, God Almighty! You never can tell. With women such as yon, you never know what you'll get left with."

*   *   *

But it was his father's homecoming on Term Nights that lay within Hugh Riddel's own remembrance, and still could move him in the minding of it.

God! But what a difference a drink and a day off had made to the man. Hard to reconcile the dour everyday father of the fields and byres with the huge genial man who stood swaying and singing in the doorway, flanked by his fellow farm-workers on Term Nights.

Her brow 'tis like the snawdrift.
Her neck 'tis like the swan.
Her face it is the fairest
That e'er the sun shone on.

And dark blue is her e'e.
And she's a' the world to me.
And for bonnie Annie Laurie
I wad lay me doon and dee!

That was another of the times when Hugh Riddel, the boy, had felt all the glamourie of manhood tugging at himself. The *Annie Lauries* and *Bonnie Peggies* of his father's songs had come across to him even then as something more than idylls of time gone past; they became the lush promises of his own future. Strange, though; strange that they should still have remained idylls when the future had become the present.

Like dew on the gowan lying
Is the fa' o' her fairy feet.
And like wind in the summer sighing.
Her voice is low and sweet!

"Keep *your* voice down, then. And come on inside the house with you. For it will be the clash of the countryside that you couldn't stand on *your* fairy feet on Term Night."

Down all the years Hugh Riddel could still call up his mother's capacity for diminishing his father. Not

even the presence of his father's fellow-workers had
ever prevented her from putting on the hurt, white face
of martyrdom. A right bad wife could ease a man's
conscience, and so set him free. But a good wife
could bind you prisoner forever, with the swaddling
bands of her goodness. God! but I had to burst myself out and free, Hugh Riddel thought. His father
had never brought himself to do likewise. For this,
his son could pity but also envy him, and saw him
still in all his huge, blustering futility.

"Well, well, woman. If everybody's tongues are
clashing about *me*, it stands to reason that they will be
leaving some other poor sinful bugger to a bit of
peace. And *that's* surely a something to be thankful
for! Come in, about then, all of you. Come on, now.
Draw your chairs up to the fire, and we'll have a bit
of a crack and a song to ourselves."

That was another of the times when Hugh Riddel
had felt insulated in a comfort of spirit. Curled up in
the kitchen bed, in the dim flicker of firelight and
lamplight. Within hand's touch of a world of men.
Yet still safe onlooker, with the voices of his father
and his father's friends droning over and round him.

Oh, never were harvests so wet and wild as those
they recollected in their cups on Term Nights. And
still miraculously ingathered. For they could see
themselves in their young years, through such a space
of time that personal identification left them altogether. And it was giants, immune to wind and

31

weather, who rode the rigs; and scythed the "in-roads" to epic harvests.

But, despite all their exaggerations, and for all his own youngness at the time, Hugh Riddel had instinctively recognised their underlying truth. It was simply that words had caricatured their thoughts. And, by God, words could do *that*, right enough. Look and touch and feel should suffice to allow you walk wordless all your days. Hugh Riddel remembered one small such instance of his own, on the farm near Stonehaven, where the hill slopes had lain under grass through living memory, till one morning on his road to school he had stood arrested, staring at the sharp gleaming coulter of the plough cutting into the hill slope and leaving the first dark furrow. That had struck him with an almost physical sense of pain. And the image of the virgin land with the gash of a wound across it had lain unvoiced in mind for a long time. Small wonder, then, that with the nowhereness of words, his father and his father's friends had grabbed them and twined them and stretched them this way and that, in a kind of anger at their impotence.

But there was the other side of it. The times when threadbare words could cast a shadow, far greater than the substance of their meaning, across your mind, mantling it for the rest of your days. A small memory too, and gleaned on a Term night.

"Oh, but he was a hard farmer to work for," God

Knows had said. "You durst never be caught
straightening your back when yon one came in sight
of you. And God knows, many's the time I have seen
myself, after ten hours' forking to the threshing mill,
bend down just to pick up some straw, knowing that
the wind would blow another in its place, when I'd
hear the sound of his footsteps."

That was when High Riddel had first known the
true meaning of physical tiredness, even before ex-
periencing it. And, ever afterwards, the ultimate
weariness was indeed just to "pick up some straw,
knowing that the wind would blow another in its
place".

But he had been infatuated by the speak of the
life on the land on those far-off Term Nights. For
those nights were Hugh Riddel's initiation into a
society to which one could only obtain membership
by right of birth. A comparatively secret society too.
One which had its being scattered unmarked on the
teacher's map at school, where Scotland was made
up of Highlands and Lowlands, mining and ship-
building, cathedral towns and university cities, and
all their world ending abruptly "over the Border".

It was his father and his father's friends who
crammed the blanks of that map on Term Nights, till
Scotland became a continent on their tongues and
famous for things that never found their way into the
Geography lesson at school. The fine tattie-growing
soil of Easter Ross. South of the Mearns where the

land was more mellow, the farmers easier, the darg lighter, and fees higher. Up Inverness way, where the last battle fought on British soil was forgotten, and only the democracy of the "folk" remembered.

"I kent a ploughman once," Dod Feary had pointed out, as impressive proof of this to his incredulous listeners, "who used to get blind drunk every Saturday night with the local Doctor, up Culloden way."

For nowhere was "Keeping one's proper place" so strictly adhered to as in our shire. Even his mother, Hugh Riddel remembered, had once commented on this:

"If the farmer's wife passes the time of day with the cottar wives, it just makes their day. Poor, silly bodies! You would think that the Lord above had looked down from Heaven, and greeted them personally, so overcome are they."

Hugh Riddel smiled at the recollection. But there was a kind of pain and protest at the heart of his amusement.

. . . Oh, Burns. Was it to suit the fine sentiments of the Edinbro' Gentry, once cursed by you, and always half despised, that you wrote such smarm as *The Cotter's Saturday Night?*

> *From scenes like these*
> *Old Scotia's grandeur springs. . . .*

The lines grued in Hugh Riddel's mind. It was

easily seen that such a poem was written by a man who ploughed his *own* furrows. Never by a fee'd ploughman. And although farm-workers' conditions had improved beyond all recognition now, Hugh Riddel's pain, though momentary, was ever recurring. It was just that no man could come into good estate free of that which and those who had preceded him.

Far more true of their way of life were the songs of his father and his father's friends on Term Night. Songs of their own countryside, composed by themselves for themselves; and having their origins in the very farms they worked on.

> *When I gaed doon to Turra Market*
> *Turra Market for to fee*
> *I met in wi' a wealthy fairmer*
> *Frae the Barnyards o' Delgaty!*

> *He promised me the twa best horse*
> *That was in a' the country roon*
> *But when I gaed hame to the Barnyards*
> *There was nothing there but skin and bone!*

It was when they reached the singing stage on Term Nights that they really tried his mother's patience. It was then that they sent her sighing "God be here" round the kitchen, and "there will be no word of this in the morning"; and, as the night advanced and the songs grew coarser, would set her to redding up the kitchen. As if by the very act she could also redd up the dirt rising round her ears. For how the men loved dirt. That which his father had always protested was "*Clean* dirt, woman!" And Hugh Riddel himself had always been in alliance with the men over this.

> *She let him in sae cannily*
> *To do the thing you ken, Jo!*
> *She chased him out syne cried him back*
> *To do it once again, Jo!*
> *But the bottom fell out o' the bed*
> *The lassie lost her maiden-head*
> *And her mither heard the din, Jo!*

It always meant some other new song for Hugh Riddel to go racing schoolwards with, the wind in his face; and a pack of loons panting behind him to hear the rest of it, syne flinging themselves face downwards on the grass with the exhaustion of their laughter, and laughing long after they had forgotten the cause. Pure laughter that, Hugh Riddel realised now, for it had needed no reason.

God! you could stand out here in the dark, and listen to the youngness of your life singing away past you there, as if it had been conceived in song. His mother had never realised it was like that with him, though. She was always protecting him from his father and his father's cronies, their songs and their talk.

"*That's* fine language to be on you all! And the bairn Hugh there, lying in his bed."

"Well! Hugh's got to find out for himself one of these fine days," his father would defend. "For fine he knows that he wasn't found at the back of a cabbage plant, as you would like him to believe!"

And fine he did know. Ever since he could remember, Hugh Riddel had discovered that sex was the great topic and the huge laugh, the joke that the farm-workers seldom tired of, and rearing itself up at all odd times in all kinds of places. The bulls serving the cows. And the stallions serving the mares. And ill-favoured Annie Coultrie, whom no man had tried to tempt for years, drawing her cardigan fierce around her shoulders, like to protect her virtue, and screeching across the steading.

There's the stallion man. Just coming up the road yonder, with that great muckle brute of a stallion. But I'm not going to put *him* up for the night. Not *me*! He can just go to the bothy for a bed, or to some woman that's his own like. For they're saying that the man has gotten as randy as that stallion he treks around the country with. They have it that no woman under sixty is safe with him now."

And the deep satirical laughter her indignation evoked in the men.

"*You'll* be safe enough then, Annie, for you'll not see sixty again. Though you was always safe enough, Annie. Even when you was sixteen!"

But there was always a quality of cruelty in the laughter evoked by sex. A quality which Hugh Riddel recognised in himself, and which was maybe contained to an even greater degree in men far beyond the parish of Caldwell. Take the war years, now, and the time when the Polish airmen were stationed over there at Balwhine. What a clash of tongues *they* had caused in the countryside. God Knows had been fair flabbergasted by their methods. His fiery denunciation of the Poles still burned in Hugh Riddel's recollection.

"The Cottage Hospital is fair full of queans with festered breasts the now! For it seems that plain fornication is just not good enough for that Polish chields. Na. Na. They've got to bite as well. And that, mark you, with all their fine polite words and ways, their kissing hands and all the rest of their palaver. Surely to God a decent man can have a quean without wanting to take bites out of her."

Laughter shook Hugh Riddel at the recollection, and metaphorically flung him face downwards on a grassy bank, thirty years away in time. But, like laughter of that kind and quality, it left him empty enough for tears. *O! My love Annie's wondrous bonnie.* It was the idyll one's spirit always wept for.

"It's when there's neither lust nor liking," his father had once confided, "that a man's marriage has got nothing." Lust nor liking. He had never heard his father use the word "love", except in song.

But it was all going to be very different with *him*. Hugh Riddel had made up his mind early about that.

"A quiet decent lass," his mother had said, approving his ultimate choice of a wife. Though, come to consider it now, Isa was not unlike what his mother had been. It was her small white quality of chastity that had first attracted Hugh Riddel. Novel enough in a time and place where there was nothing for the young to do in the little free time they had to themselves but "Away to the whin bushes, and into it", as the older men still described it.

Strange that he had been so deluded. The onlookers weren't.

"Isa Mavor! Yon mim-mouthed quean. God, Riddel, but I'd imagine yon one would be on the cold side to bed with, if her thin pernickity walk is anything to go by."

And his own resentment of their unsolicited opinions.

"There are other ways of judging a woman. It's not a heifer that you're sizing up."

They had been right, though. Hugh Riddel had to admit that to himself. Times he had felt like contradicting his daughter, Helen, when she came home weekends from her work in a Youth Centre in the Town, with words on the tip of her tongue, like labels, ready to be stuck on to all human faults and frailties. As though the correct word for them could cure them. Words like Delinquency, Hereditary, Environment, Behaviour Patterns. Whiles he felt just like boring through that wall of words with which Helen had surrounded both herself and her vocation, and blowing them sky high with the anger that would be over him.

"Take murder now, Helen. Aye murder. Whiles I just feel like murdering your mother with my two bare hands. And not even for the big things that are wrong between us. Just, God help me, for the smallest thing of all. Like times when your mother's standing silent by the window. And you know the look that's on her face, by the back of her head. And I go clattering through to the sink to wash my face, making a racket to cover up the wordlessness that falls between us. Syne putting my head round the corner of the scullery door to see if the din I've made has stirred into movement, though Hell let loose itself, could scare do that! My eye takes in the whole of her – against its will. But when it reaches the stockings wrinkling round her legs, it's then that I could kill her. For the disgust that's on me for having chosen such a woman. What name have they given to *that* in your Youth Centre, Helen? What word is there for the wrinkled stocking that can incline a man to think of murder?"

And, since doubtless Helen would have had the cool clipped reply, but never the answer, he had never deigned to put the question to her.

God! but it was damnable. A man could slip his boot off in the bottling shed, and hold his bare foot out for inspection – his *foot* – that most ridiculous intimate part of him, urging his workmates:

"Take a look at that, now. At that great brute of a bunion! What would you do with a muckle thing like that? It has given me agony for weeks. Pure agony just!"

And advice would pour forth thick and fast, for it would seem that all the dairy workers would have had a bunion the like, at some time or another, so it would prove complaint but common enough.

But there was never time, nor place, nor person to whom you could confide this deeper agony:

"Was it this way with you when you got married? Did your wife lie in a cold clam beside you? And for her youngness did you restrain yourself, feeling but brute and guilty. Yet hoping the time would come – and soon – when hugging and kissing were not enough even for her. And when time came, it was reluctant. And as time passed, became as cold as charity bequeathed from duty, so that your hunger for it left you altogether; and appetite itself turned to distaste, so that even were it *offered* to you now, you couldn't stomach it."

That too, if aired within the bottling shed, might prove to be complaint but common enough, though one that was for Riddel beyond enduring.

It came back to him now, as near as yesterday,

his father's voice, bewildered and defeated: "What would you make of women folk, Hugh? I can never say a bonnie wordie to your mother but she tells me I'm drunk. And maybe she's right at that of it. For it is only when I am drunk that the words come to me, and the notion takes me.

And his mother's bitter response:

"The trouble with you is you should have married some great roaring quean who was more your like."

But it was senseless standing here, regretting. Hugh Riddel realised that. For regret neither eased an old pain, nor taught you how to avoid a new one. Live and learn, that's what they said. He lived all right, but he just never seemed to learn, since experience itself but taught you not to make the *same* mistake twice. And sometimes, not even that.

. . . Darklands' milk lorry, roaring in the distance, was taking the Tienland Corner now, its headlights picking up the landmarks on the road, lifting them up into the light and dropping them down into the darkness again. Hugh Riddel still stood, reluctant to brace himself for the ordeal of facing the Dairy. For, although the degree of a man's fault is known only in part, even to himself, the exact opinions of that fault can be accurately gauged in the eyes and attitudes of his fellow-men.

Not that he cared a tinker's curse what his fellow-workers thought of him, Hugh Riddel assured him-

self. Far from it. He had always been indifferent to
their opinions. And his knowledge of them had en-
sured this attitude. Good or bad, top dog was always
top dog to them. Oh, it might bite them and they'd
yelp out with pain; but the instant it barked out in
more genial salutation, they would come panting,
their tongues hanging out, and their tails wagging.
It was only when one no longer proved to be top
dog that apprehension might well set in. For then
the pack – always bold on top of their own midden
– would set about you, tearing you to pieces.

The thought of that angered Hugh Riddel, but
braced him into movement. Damn them! Damn
them all. He would go up into the dairy as if nothing
had happened. He would supervise the loading of
that milk lorry, as if last Friday was still some future
date on the calender above the bottling machine,
circled in red, for nothing more important than a
reminder to "Order more Quart Bottles". And he
would do that, too. By God he would! For, at this
moment, he was still Hugh Riddel, Head Dairyman,
Darklands.

The conviction took such a hold of him that the
need for haste left him altogether. And it was with
the slow loping stride of habit that he began to make
his way up to the dairy, pausing only to interpret the
night.

There was an orange glow round the last quarter
of the moon, and the Mother Tap of Soutar Hill

was hidden in the mist that was starting to come down. The smell of ground frost rose dankly up from the nether park. Real Judas weather, and this now into February. Still, Darklands would cope with all that in its own good time.

*　　　　*　　　　*

The Dairy was loud with the speculation of last Friday night. For it was the kind of night which should have found itself head-lined in the Sunday paper, although it hadn't done so, to the chagrin of God Knows.

"Bloody near a murder!" he shouted across to the Plunger, above the din of the bottling machine.

"Forbye a try at suicide, and the Lunatic Asylum!"

"*Not* the Lunatic Asylum!" Lil Jarvis contradicted from her stool in front of the bottling machine.

"Ambroggan House. A *private* Mental Hospital for Helen Riddel, if you please."

"Whatever name it goes by, its purpose is the same," God Knows snapped, nettled by the sarcasm in Lil's voice. He had never had very much meed for any of the Riddel breed – except Hugh Riddel's father – but he had even less for Lil Jarvis; always running himself and the other cattlemen off their feet with her perpetual cry of "more milk for bottling".

"And all kinds of queer going-ons in between,"

44

God Knows continued, ignoring Lil, and deliberately turning his attention to the Plunger.

"Goings-on that you and me will never likely get to the bottom of," he added regretfully, "for God only knows *what* the world is coming to."

God Knows had been speculating on what the world was coming to for the best part of sixty years. A narrow enough speculation, since it was simply the neighbouring parishes outwith Caldwell that gave him such cause for anxiety. Caldwell itself was the promised land; its inhabitants the chosen people, though just as wilful whiles as the Israelites themselves. Until now, that was, for the world still knew nothing of Caldwell's fall from grace.

"There was not a single word about it in any of the Sunday papers," God Knows confirmed. "Just the usual tell of a puckle queans in the South being followed, or offered lifts in cars, syne kicking up a terrible rumpus about it all afterwards."

"*I* have never been followed in all my life," Lil boasted from the bottling machine, as though this was some hard-won personal triumph. "And I have walked about the earth for a good few years now. But I never ran into anything worse than myself on a dark night!"

It would have greatly surprised God Knows and the other dairy workers had Lil ever done so. Still, God Knows felt it more prudent to let her avowal go unchallenged.

"They must be a terrible lot, thae queans in the South," was all he could think of saying in reply. "They must just all go about asking for it!"

"It's my opinion" – Lil clamped her conclusion firmly down with the bang of her bottling lever – "my honest opinion – that Hugh Riddel, to say nothing of yon stuck-up daughter of his, Helen, with all her fine college education, and her eyes looking at you over the top of yon specs she wears, as if you were some kind of thing she didn't see very often – it's my opinion that they just all got what they've been asking for, for a long, long time."

"They say it's still just touch and go with the Riddel quean, though," the Plunger ventured, reluctant to condemn one who might be at death's door.

"*She'll* survive," Lil, plagued by no such ethics herself, assured the men. "Yon wish washy molloching kind of creature always does. And as for yon Charlie Anson, he's been asking for a good hiding all his life. And deed, that was the only good thing in the whole sorry business. They say that Hugh Riddel made a bonnie mess out of him!"

"Deed aye." Despite himself, God Knows found himself in complete agreement with Lil on this point. "For I never yet looked on yon buck teeth of Anson's but they put me in mind of a rabbit sitting up on its hunkers and laughing at something or other. But Anson will laugh no more like yon, for they say that Hugh Riddel didna leave a tooth in his head."

"There's *one* thing, though," the Plunger straightened himself up from the tank to give his reflections full weight, "and *it's* certain. Sue Tatt hasn't gone into mourning over Friday night's affair, for I saw her at the Grocer's van, just yestreen, as large as life yonder and twice as sinful, chewing the fat and skirling away like a sixteen-year-old, with the new vanman that's on the round."

"I never could understand that Sue Tatt business at all," God Knows pondered. "It was just fair beyond my comprehension. You would have thought that a man like Hugh Riddel would have been a bit more choosy, Sue being such a byword in the Parish, like."

"There's no mystery to that at all," the Plunger said. "You know what Burns had to say about it? I'll tone it down a bit – for Lil's sake, there. It wouldn't do to shock our Lil's maidenly modesty. A desperate man has no conscience, and a willing woman has no objection. That's what Burns said. In stronger language, though. But that, if you ask me, was all there was between Sue Tatt and Hugh Riddel."

"Maybe that, then," God Knows conceded, "though I'll wager you that Hugh Riddel will give Sue the Soldier's farewell from now on."

"He'll have no other option," Lil concluded, "for

I can see Darklands showing Riddel down the road real smartlike for Friday night's work. For Darklands will not have very much option either, what with him being an Elder of the Kirk, forbye a County Councillor."

"I wouldn't take a bet on it." God Knows spoke out of authority of long acquaintance with Darklands – the farm, and the farmer. "For I mind when I was fee'd to come home to Darklands here. And that wasn't yesterday. That was before Darklands' herd was built up, when he was just pleitering about with a bit of mixed farming and, say, a forty fifty stots; for even then, he had a kind of passion for kye. No T.T. Testing *then*, Plunger. You just had to take your chance with weedy milk and all the rest of it. And it was in the days when we were allowed to keep our own hens. In those days, Plunger, you could judge a farmer by his attitude to his cottars' hens. If he said, 'No Hens', then you could be pretty certain that you had gone and bonded yourself not only to a suspicious man, but to a man as mean as cat's dirt as well. Anyhow, the first question Darklands asked me was if I kept hens of my own. 'Aye,' I admitted, 'I've got a two three hennies.' He pondered on that for a while syne. 'Well, well,' says he at last, 'I'll tell you what I'll do. I'll allow you, along with your Fee, a pucklie oats for your two three hennies!' I was just about to thank him for the favour, but he wouldn't hear of it. 'Not at all,' he

48

said. 'I'll allow you the oats to save you the bother of getting out of your bed in the middle of the night, and slinking up to the barn to help yourself.' So you *see*, you can never tell what airt the wind will blow with a man who reasons like that! And don't you forget this either," God Knows continued, fired by his listeners' attention, "don't you forget that it was Hugh Riddel's father who was Darklands' first cattleman when he started to build up his herd. They kind of built it up together. It was the only job that old Riddel had ever lasted in. He was never sent down the road on that job, for he was a grand cattleman. By God, he was that! It was never old Riddel's *work* that was wanting. He could tell when a cow was in heat, when the bull itself would still be standing wondering about it! And he could have clippit a cow blindfold, going over her flanks as surely as he could always find his way home on Term Nights, and him as full as a distiller's cask!"

"Get to hell out of it! Back to your byre." Hugh Riddel's voice sent Lil's stool swivelling round in front of the bottling machine, and set the Plunger's back bending over the tank again. The lorry men sauntered in with the large deliberate assurance of men who had every right to be there anyhow.

"I said back to your byre," Riddel repeated to God Knows, who, lacking his fellow-workers' speed of camouflage, still stood staring blankly.

"Aye, aye surely, Mr Riddel." It was only when

he reached his byre that God Knows reproved himself for not taking a firmer stand. "There was me *Mistering* him!" he confided to the Third Cattleman. "Mr Riddel," says I, "and the man accepted it, as if it was just his due as usual. You would think that Hugh Riddel would walk humbly enough now, after last Friday night's happenings."

*   *   *

Last Friday night had started off like any other Friday night in Caldwell – furious with activity.

Up at Ambroggan House, the younger nurses coming off day duty made hasty applications for late-night passes, and sprawling on each others' beds indulged in sartorial barter. Not without reason were the nurses the best-dressed girls in all the parish. And, having acquired a Late Night for themselves, and finally decided Which of Whose to wear, were puzzled now by how to use both gains to best advantage: to the Half Crown Hop in Caldwell Hall, on the pillion of a Vespa with some male nurse as hard up as themselves; or to the Guinea Dinner Dance in the Town, in the front seat of a Consul, with some farmer's son who – sure as death – would, at some time or another before the night was over, suggest, and even attempt, a bodily transference to the back seat of the car.

Their older colleagues, contemptous now of such acrobatic feats, were just content to sink into easy

chairs, slip off their shoes, and proffer their advice –
rejected either way.

The nurses coming on Night Duty cast eyes half
filled with sleep upon the world outside their bedroom windows, took yet another vow that never
again would they skip morning sleep to have their
hair done, not if they walked the world the rest of
their days looking like Meg, the "parish patient"
who did the laundry. And yet one other vow they
reinforced, as the isolated landmarks of Caldwell
penetrated their half-awakened consciousness, to
apply forthwith for a transfer to the Hospital's
branch in the Town, for in all four years between
taking her Prelims and sewing the strings of Charge
Nurse on her cap, Caldwell was surely the most forsaken dump a girl could land herself in.

While all the afternoon the daft Dominie, their
patient on parole, had sat on Soutar Hill, certain it
was the mountain of Gilboah, with neither dew upon
it, nor fields of offerings.

It was the night the Misses Lennox, and other like
ladies of the parish, slipped from small houses with
long names on their gates, armed with damp sand-
wiches, and clinging trails of jasmine, just in bloom.
Then, drawing fur tippets firm around their necks,
sniffed the night air and bowed their heads against
the oncoming wind before stepping warily Kirkwards, decrying the noise and fumes of passing cars,
hell bent for Dugald's Road-house, and all New

Rich, and ostentatiousness in every form, as well as
couples who boldly strode the road together, hand
in hand, pausing to watch the lights go up in distant
farmhouses, acclaiming each and recognising all.
Then stopping to kiss each other under the moon,
and in the sight of the Misses Lennox; laughing
about it to high Heaven, as if love itself were but a
joke. For Miss Lennox had never thought love so,
while Miss Maud even doubted whether it was love
at all, or just one more manifestation of why Caldwell
had the highest illegitimacy rate in all the County.

The Misses Lennox felt themselves to be the guardians of Caldwell by right of birth. And yet –
despite this accident, and for all their years within
Caldwell – could not have told you from which direction the wind was rising now, nor in which quarter
the moon above them lay. They only recognised full
moons, and rapturously acclaimed the huge red
harvest ones; could never discern quarters, nor yet
appreciate small blue elusive February moons like
this, which seemed to them but accident of light and
cloud.

Their thoughts turned Kirkwards now, and to the
men in their own lives, the Minister, visiting mission-
aries home on furlough – and God. Perhaps God
most of all. Though He, of course, was more than
man, but yet fulfilling their emotional needs, without
man's nuisance value.

And thinking so, the Misses Lennox remembrance

fell, while their wrath rose on one such man. It was just the man's presumption roused their ire.

A farm-worker to be asked – far worse consent – to give the speech, and toast "The Immortal Memory", at the Burns' Supper the other night, an honour usually reserved for Colonels retired, or Ministers, active and passive. The insolence of the man, Head Dairyman at Darklands, Hugh Riddel by name, to stand barefaced up and tell *them* that half the people sitting there, listening to and praising Burns' songs and poems, would have no more meed for Burns himself if he were to settle down amongst them tomorrow, than the "unco guid" had for him in Mauchline in his own day.

To dismiss the people of Caldwell like that was bad enough, but the man had gone on to do something worse than that: he had deprived them of the comfort of myth; had flung, as it were, all the little china statues of Highland Mary off their mantlepieces and left them lying in broken pieces.

Nor had he left them with their other substitute for comfort intact, their *Bonnie Jean.* In places like Mauchline and Caldwell, he had claimed, Burns would have been left with little choice but to marry Jean Armour – Oh, but aye! For any man could live after being worried, but no man could live after being disgraced. So, no particular credit to Burns for *that* marriage. And, having married him, Jean Armour would have had little choice but to put up with Burns. For, wasn't that just the way of it in country places? In all their years in Caldwell, now, had any one of them ever known of a farm-worker, or even a farmer for that of it, going and getting divorced? Nor was it their religion which imposed this attitude upon them, for there wasn't a Catholic within fifty miles of them.

There were, the man had said, plenty women of Jean Armour's sort who would have been willing enough to share Burns' name, his bed and his board, but he had needed something much more than that in a wife; he had needed the impossible. To have one foot on the front step of the castle, and the other trailing behind on the dunghill, and never both together, was just about the loneliest thing that could ever befall a man, and the woman wasn't born who could have bridged this gap with Burns. But, mind you, that had never prevented Burns from searching for her, and even glimpsing her fleeting reflection in the faces of all women; personifying her in the love songs he wrote to all the Peggies, Marys, Jeans and Nancys, for they but fuelled some flame already lit. And the self-same thing applied to all his nature lyrics. Had Burns never set eyes on the daisy, the briar, or the canna white ablown, he still would have sung for "some wee sma' flower, whose seed was never sown", knowing that the herb which cannot be found will not bring relief.

Oh, but it had been galling to find Hugh Riddel's

Immortal Memory printed in full in the national press. ONE PLOUGHMAN SPEAKS OF ANOTHER – ROBERT BURNS, the heading had said, instead of as usual tucked away in a column of the local paper under CALDWELL EVENTS, where everybody who was anybody in Caldwell would have been certain of seeing their own names in print. But not one word about the Colonel who had piped the haggis in, nor the Dominie who had "addressed" it, or the Minister who had said the Burns' Grace over it. Not a mention of "The Ladies" – which had included the Misses Lennox – "who had helped to make the event such an unqualified success, by working like Trojans behind the scenes", as their functions were normally described. Not even a mention of the "fine rendering of *The Bonnie Lass O' Ballochmyle*, by Miss McCombie of The Whins". Though quite unknown to the Misses Lennox, Hugh Riddel himself had observed on this to God Knows on their way home from the Burns Supper:

"Miss McCombie will now render *The Bonnie Lass O' Ballochmyle*, said the Chairman. And the Chairman was just about right at that. For yon bloody woman nearly tore The Bonnie Lass apart!"

Not a mention of anyone at all, except a local farm-worker whom nobody even knew, nor, as far as the Misses Lennox were concerned, wished to know either. It just went to show. You never could trust the uneducated. Take that miner turned lay preacher, who had addressed them up in the Kirk Hall last month, accusing *them* of being quite capable of crucifying Christ again because they lacked recognition. A recollection which rankled particularly with the Misses Lennox, for it was one of their great dreams and small hopes that, for His Second Coming, Christ would choose Caldwell, convinced that they would be the first to recognise Him, after a lifetime acquaintance with Holman Hunt's *Light of World* in their front parlour.

And so they talked till other like ladies of the parish, who lurked in waiting, pounced out upon them from small side roads or clumps of whins, giggling together with feared surprise. Like ghosts of girls.

*   *   *

At this time, too, the farm-workers' wives were taking the opposite direction to the Woman's "Rural", their tongues as sharp, their thoughts as bright and bitter as the jars of marmalade clanking in their baskets. For this was Marmalade Competition Night; two classes – Rough and Fine. These were no guardians of Caldwell, but content merely as critics, an easier role, and altogether safer. Yet, not one amongst them but knew how mornings were, earlier than you have ever known them: how in such isolated hours the well-trod path towards their byres was like some track in an uncharted world; how when darkness fell, overtaking them on the road, a lamplit farmhouse five miles away was surer guide than bright Orion and all the mariners' stars. Small wonder, then, their tongues wagged wild, in general observation, for the small particular was ever without voice.

Now! What did this one make of Hugh Riddel's Immortal Memory, a week ago tonight, up in the Hall? They had not quite got beyond the fact that one of themselves had been allowed voice at last, and were inclined to warm themselves contentedly at the thought; till God Know's wife began to scatter straws of doubt within their minds. " 'Twas just the kind of thing could make a man go all above himself," she vowed, "not, mind you, that Hugh Riddel had ever had other than a fine conceit of himself – and that kind needs just a little push to send them clean off their balance."

"Take Charlie Anson now, and for example," the Plunger's wife remembered. "Until yon creature was appointed Treasurer of the Farm-workers' Union, who would have ever given him a second thought? And now the man was taking himself seriously. Just you observe him. Speaking English! As if he had never learned a word of Scots, or else was shamed of it!"

"He has even given his bonnet the go-by," Lil recalled, "and taken to wearing a hat instead, lifting it to every conceivable woman he met on the road, just to prove that he knew what to do with a hat."

"Though, God help us," as the Plunger's wife pointed out, in an attempt to modify resentment, "the creature looks just as like a weasel under the hat, as ever he looked under the bonnet! And, when he lifts his hat to *me*, I just look through it, and him too."

"Oh, but Charlie Anson does worse than that," as God Knows' wife reminded them. "He not only speaks English, he's beginning to think he discovered Scots as well. Yon talk he gave at the Cultural Society – Words Your Heritage, he cried it, and didn't even know he was being insulting. As if it was *us* who had forsaken our Scots' tongue, and not himself! I will say this much for Hugh Riddel; you may not like him, but you cannot despise him. And another thing, did you notice that when Hugh Riddel was saying *Holy Willie's Prayer* that night at the Burns' Supper, did you notice, he never once took his eyes off Charlie Anson?"

"God!" Lil remembered, "I even began to feel sorry for Charlie Anson himself, sitting squirming yonder under Hugh Riddel's glower."

"Yon was a sight pleased me right fine," the Plunger's wife admitted. "But I'll wager you this much, Hugh Riddel would have done a damned sight more than glower at Charlie Anson, if he'd had any inkling that Anson's taken up with his daughter. It's an odd thing, but I'll wager, too, Riddel will be the last man in Caldwell to hear anything about that."

"You always are the last to hear anything about your own," Lil pointed out. "And I, for one, wouldn't take five pounds to be the first to tell Hugh Riddel about Anson and his daughter."

"Nor me, either," God Knows' wife agreed. "But I would give ten pounds to be the first to see his face after somebody else has told him."

"Even so," the Plunger's wife felt that the issue was getting out of perspective, "the pot can never call the kettle black. At least Hugh Riddel's daughter is single. She can please herself, as can Charlie Anson for that of it. Though the woman who would ever look twice at him must be pretty desperate."

"But Helen Riddel *is* desperate," was Lil's opinion. "for all her education, and all the speak of the brains she's gotten. She's a poor white shelpit creature. She takes after the mother in that respect."

"I just wonder what Isa Riddel would have thought of her man's Immortal Memory, if she'd been there to hear it," God Knows' wife pondered.

"All Hugh Riddel's women-folk were better away that night." Lil's emphatic largess consigned a harem to him. "Though I can tell you this much: if Sue Tatt had been yonder to hear him describe her like as 'necessary' to Burns, she would have sent him away with a flea in his lug."

"Still and on," the Plunger's wife recalled, "the way Hugh Riddel spoke that night, about Burns' farms at Lochlea and Ellisland, there was a while yonder I got the feeling that they were just two farms lying somewhere under Soutar Hill here. And that Hugh Riddel had ploughed every acre of them himself."

> *"Come ony man at all*
> *And tak me frae my faither"*

Lil started to sing, desirous suddenly of freeing herself of her companions, and strode away down into the night on her own.

> *"For it's O dearie me!*
> *What shall I dae*
> *If I die an auld maid in a garret."*

"Wheesht, you now!" the Plunger's wife admonished, catching up on Lil. "Look see!" she whispered mysteriously, grabbing Lil's arm and holding her firm captive till the others caught up with them before revealing the mystery. "Look see! There's a light just gone up in Sue Tatt's bedroom. Business as usual there, on a Friday night!"

*   *   *

"Fiona!" Sue Tatt shouted upstairs in warning, to her eldest daughter. "If you go mucking up all my new cleaned bedroom, I'll land you one. You'll go flying straight through the wall. And that's a promise!"

Having got this off her chest, Sue made her way

back to the kitchen again, pausing in the doorway as though she were some complete stranger come to pay a visit to herself, and, standing there, took in every aspect of her newly turned-out room. Sue, a woman of many parts, was equal to many roles, and Fridays always brought out the house-proud in her.

True, her household would rough it contentedly enough all the rest of the week, when Sue would be absorbed in some other role, though she would always justify her muddle to anyone who crossed her threshold uninvited, with the dubious welcome, "You're just about the last one I was looking for. But come on away inside. The clartier the cosier! Or so they say" – accompanied by a slap on the back that would have flung you flat on your face if you hadn't been expecting it. But, when the pendulum swung the *other* way, as now, a tiny speck of dust in any corner of her house was enough to send Sue up in smoke, and was more than a little unfair on her family, who could never quite adjust themselves to the suddenness of their mother's change of role. And doubly unfair tonight, when Sue was combining two roles.

She would let days pass on end, giving her face a lick and a promise, and her hair a rough redd through. But today a sudden beautifying spasm had seized her; a visit to the Town and Woolworths had become a Must. Descending on the cosmetic counter, Sue had bought up everything that promised anything: a Face Pack which "erased tell-tale wrinkles", a Highlight Rinse which "brought out hidden golden glints", a lipstick which "carried a breath of Spring". And, miser-like, Sue was now preparing to lock herself away in the bathroom, with all her little packages, and looking forward to lying, soaking herself leisurely, and reading the instructions on her Beauty Aids as lovingly as if they were the word of God – though with more faith.

"I'll be in the bathroom if I'm wanted," she reminded Fiona. "And don't any of you lot go mucking all my place up," she warned again.

"Forget it, Mam," Fiona advised casually from the bedroom. "Don't let it go and get your wick."

"I'll tell you what does get my wick" – Sue turned to survey her kitchen again – "and that's just the sight of a pair of sharny boots lying on my new-brushed rug. You would think," she added in pained protest, "that we all lived in a pig-sty."

"We do, too." Young Beel dodged Sue's aim, but gave her the cue for another role.

"I work my fingers to the bone for you all," she complained, "slaving to bring you up, and that's all the thanks I get." She made her way to the bathroom almost tearfully, remembering now that she was "a widow woman, bringing up a young family, all on her own."

And indeed it was a kind of truth. Though Sue did whiles confuse the names of the mythical husbands who had widowed her, certain it was that she worked with a fair degree of regularity to bring up her bairns. "*Drag* them up" was Caldwell's private interpretation of her efforts. But, then, Caldwell was seldom charitable towards its own. For though they accepted Sue as their own, they condoned neither Sue nor themselves for this acceptance.

The role of Self Supporting Widow was dear to Sue's heart. Mounting her bicycle two or three times a week to do the wash for surrounding farmers' wives, Sue was aware of the heightened interest she aroused both in them and in their daily helps, who were forever making some excuse to pop into the wash-house for a news with Sue. And the self-same thing with the farm-workers' wives. Sue Tatt was well aware that their attitude to herself veered between superiority and a kind of envy. And their approach towards her was transparency itself.

Meeting any one of them alone on the Ambroggan road it would simply be as housewife to housewife: newsing together of this and that; the cost of food, exchanging a recipe maybe, or a cleaning hint. In such moments, Sue would become so enthusiastic over the preserving qualities of bees' wax and turpentine, that she would deceive even herself and, mounting her bicycle, would take down the road a glow of goodness over her, and the assurance within her – I, Sue Tatt, am just an ordinary housewife after all. And what is more, I am accepted as such by the Plunger's wife.

When Sue Tatt ran into a group of farm-workers' wives, things took a different turn altogether.

"Aye! But it's another fine night, again," the Plunger's wife would shoot out of the side of her mouth in hurried passing, the remembered mutual addiction to bees' wax and turpentine simply forcing the salutation out of her, while the other wives would just keep going, their gaze fixed steadily on the road ahead, their mouths clamped down in firm disapproval. Such an attitude always had the effect of bringing out the worst in Sue towards woman-kind – "A drab-like lot! All gone to seed. Not one amongst them would have seen their feet if they hadn't been all gripped in with brassieres and stays": while she, Sue Tatt, could stand, and sometimes did, as now, as firm mother-naked as other women in all their harness; and standing so, she would think, "Oh, the pity of it! And the waste. To grow old. And there's the whole wide world. And all of them that's in it. And I have never seen the world. Nor half of them that's in it. And what is *more* the pity is that *they* have never seen *me* so!"

Sue would have stripped herself at any time, and just for that. The way a child might rush from school, its crayoned drawing held aloft, and shouting, "Look what I've got. It's all my own!" . . . And, just as the praise of some loving observer would ring in its mind for a long time after, so would some lover's praise, when he himself and all his intimacy were long forgotten, bell in Sue's mind – "God, Sue! But you're a bonnie woman right enough."

It was when Sue Tatt ran into two wives on the road that she really came into her own, for they held the fallacy that two could keep a secret. And, having taken the risk of a friendly encounter with Sue Tatt, two wives would become bolder still, skipping hastily over the polite preliminaries like bairns, weather and neighbours, till at last they landed warily but with relief on basic ground; drawing gradually from the well of Sue's reputed experience. . . . For men were just a perfect nuisance – wasn't that so, now? My goodness me! No wonder women always aged much quicker than their menfolk, considering all they had to put up with, one way or another. A man could go on being a man till he dropped into his grave; but a woman had to call a halt, sometime or other. "Oh, it was all right when you were young and daft," the Plunger's wife had once confessed. "Though even then," she had admitted, "I got to just wanting my good night's sleep. And now, to tell the truth, it's gotten like a cup of cold water."

Oh, but to tell truth was always so much easier than to *be* truth. At least, Sue Tatt had found that so; for she met so many sweet deceptions in herself, and each seemed genuine truth. As in times like that, when Sue would find herself in entire agreement with the wives; with, all the time, the other

side of it badgering her inwardly for a hearing –
"But I never felt like that about a man, in all my
born days. Well, maybe I did. But only once or
twice. And even then, I always managed to put a
face on it. For I could never let any man feel that he
was other than the best man ever." Sue knew instinctively that a man in bed was as vulnerable as his
own nakedness, and that only by covering his failure
for him, could she reveal her own completeness.

"There are some men, though," she had once
assured Lil and the Plunger's wife – only because she
felt she owed them some little comfort and confidence
for all that they had confided in her – "There are
some men, though," Sue had informed them, "and I
have met one or two of them, that whiles feel the
same way about it all as you and me. They go so off
themselves when it's all over, that they could just
cut their throats."

Still and on, it was fine to be looked upon as something of a woman of the world, but overburdening
whiles, and more like myth than truth; then it was
finer to dissolve the burden in the wash-tub, for the
sight of their washing blowing high and white along
the lines seldom failed to produce the comment from
the farmers' wives:

"Let Sue Tatt be what she likes. One thing is sure.
She never fails to hang out a bonnie white washing!"

The same thing when they sent for her to help out
with the spring cleaning.

"I never found anybody could get the grain of that wood as white as you can scrub it, Sue," Kingorth's wife had confessed to her just the other week. And coming from Kingorth's wife that was praise, for she was a tight woman, and had she been a ghost, would have grudged giving you a fright.

Such praise was sweet to Sue, for she cared. At least, one of the many parts of her cared. So often Sue Tatt felt the conflicting burden of all her various potentialities bearing down on her. For Oh, but it was a terrible thing to have within you the power to be a plain woman or a beauty, a slut or house-proud, a respectacle body or a light of love. All of which Sue had been at some time, and could be at another, for she always grasped thc immediate potential.

"From now on," she had vowed, under the impetus of Kingorth's wife's praise, "from now on, I'm always going to clean my own little house as thoroughly as I clean other folks' big houses." And she did – for nearly a week. A week in which she almost drove her family mad; confiding sadly to Fiona, when the cleaning mood had deserted her:

"Do you know something, Fiona? I could be one of the most house-proud women in all Caldwell, if I just wasn't *Me!*"

It was true too. And Fiona, although she was only fourteen, understood the truth of it. Fiona was the only one of her children that Sue Tatt really liked; and then simply as one human being likes another.

She had named her daughter, even before she was
born, after the heroine of the serial she had been
perusing – a favourite occupation of Sue in her
carrying times.

"Fiona" – for that dark, willowy girl who strode
the heathery hills of Scottish "Family Fiction".
Tweed clad and windswept. Her head flung back.
Her eyes always "set wide apart and grey" –
scanning the far horizons of loch and hill, against
whose background stood the ancient but fast-decay-
ing House of the noble but impoverished laird, loved
by and at last won by Fiona, despite all the intrigues
of that wealthy London blonde, who never really
cared about each stick and stone of the Ancient
House. Not as Fiona did, her eyes set wide apart and
grey.

It was some flaw in Sue Tatt's nature, made her
accept Fiona – a flaw she shared with many of her
like. Even those in Caldwell who had never known
their Scotland so, preferred their image of it thus – a
fable-flowering land. But, even so, their need of the
"Rowan tree" was such, it could cause the antrin
bush to bloom unpruned within their minds. Only
an alien, and then perhaps out of a need as urgent as
their own, had ever attempted to deprive them of
their illusions.

Even God Knows himself could laugh about that,
now. "Yon Italian prisoner of war was one I'll
never forget. For Oh, but he had a right ill will to

Scotland. 'Nothing for look,' was always yon one's cry. 'In Scotland. Nothing for look. Tatties, Turnips. Rain and Wind. And no Divertiment. In Italy now! Plenty for look. Plenty Sun. Plenty Divertiment. Plenty plenty sun.' God Almighty. The way he spoke about that country of his was enough to set you thinking that the sun itself had a hard time of it getting around to get its blink in anywhere else on the face of the earth. According to yon one, it just bided in Italy. Aye, but he had a right sore grudge against Scotland. Still, like the Poles, he apparently found our women much to his liking. For I never saw a man so set on women. He had even gotten the length of teaching Sue Tatt Italian. And whatten a waste yon was. Sue could have understood what he was seeking in any tongue! Still, if his taste in countries was anything like his taste in women, Scotland lost nothing at all through his opinion of it."

But there had been those whose tastes had been worth taking all the care in the world for. Sue Tatt remembered that as she stood surveying the result of all her beautifying efforts in the bathroom mirror. It had taken a Second World War to bring Sue one tithe of the admiration which she had always felt was her due.

The curious thing about wars was that you were born in the remembrance of your parents' wars, and grew up within their constant recollections of an age, alluring as myth, "Before the War", so that you got the feeling it were better never to have been born at all than to live in the dull eras "After the War" when "Times have changed", and always "For the worst".

Sue Tatt had reached her prime during the Second World War. She now knew why the period of one's life, lived through wartime, never became relegated to the past, and, though foreshadowing the future, stood in the present, like the Celtic Cross in front of Caldwell's Old Established Church, erected to "The Memory of the Men of This Parish" who had fallen in battles as near in time and far in distance as the Dardanelles and Libya. Despite that, there still was room for the names of men who might fall in future battles, since war was never the countryman's first urgency nor last loyalty. A glance at the names on the Celtic Cross would have convinced you that, by and large, it was the countryside's artisans who "fell" – its labourers and tradesmen, and sometimes farmers' only sons, not old enough for their first heritage, side by side with crofters' younger sons who had none, since the croft ever provided for but one heir.

Maybe the flatness of "After the War" was but in natural contrast to its years of heightened tempo. Sue Tatt could see it all, as clear as yesterday, without today impinging. The first hot flush of patriotism. "All in it Together." China and Russia swinging into their orbit. Aid for them both. Knitting Bees, plain and purl; socks and balaclavas; picking up dropped stitches side by side with the

Misses Lennox, and Miss McCombie of The Whins, while Colonel McCombie, resurrected from retirement, manœuvred up on Soutar Hill with a platoon of Tractormen and Cattlemen who formed Home Guard. The sudden prestige of men in uniform, particularly their own regiment, the Gordon Highlanders. But, though you sang *Scots Wha Hae* and *Highland Laddie*, the paradox remained: the soldier, except in times of war, in moments of high sentimental fervour, in retrospect or in song, was regarded as the lowest form of life. "Where's my Mam?" . . . "She's run off with a Sodger!"

In peacetime, few girls kept company with soldiers. Sue Tatt herself had drawn the line at them, and had hitherto ignored all mating calls from Kilties. This prejudice may have had its roots in "old, unhappy far-off things", when paternity claims could be avoided by the simple expedient of enlisting. Certain it was that a strong prejudice against the soldier prevailed in country places; until wars came, of course. And then the girl not clinging to the arms of a soldier became an oddity, and an object of pity.

Sue Tatt herself had clung to not a few. The Fusiliers, when the boast on everyone's tongue was "We're going to hang out our washing on the Siegfried Line". The Tank Corps, when the prophecy was "There'll be bluebirds over the the white cliffs of Dover". And when the war was in its closing stages, Sue had vowed to the music in the Sergeants' Mess

"This is my lovely day, this the day I will remember the day I am dying".

When the first high tension of war had passed, Caldwell had settled down again to minding its own business. For its business was a total war effort – or so the Government ruled, by bringing out the Stand Still Order, which forbade all in reserved occupations to leave their jobs. But, since your born farm-worker would never have dreamt of doing so anyhow, the Stand Still Order was not only superfluous, but unsettling! As the Plunger had observed at the time, "It just never dawned on me before to leave Darklands. But then I suppose I always knew I could leave, if I so desired. And that's how it should be! I don't like the idea of this Stand Still Order. I don't like it at all."

Men who had even less control of themselves, or more within themselves, saw in the Order something against which they could test their initiative, and left their jobs on the land for no other reason than to prove it could be done. But, by and large, Caldwell had settled down again, and subsidies began to roll in – subsidies for bull calves and potatoes. Farmworkers' wages began to rise, and with them their status. The Two Term Days of the year became a thing of the past. No longer could the townsman, half affectionately, half contemptuously, instantly recognise the "Country Geordie" walking his streets, for the farm-workers' uniform – navy blue suit and bonnet – began to disappear, too. Nor was such prosperity confined to farmers and their workers. Even the tinkers wandering the countryside began to benefit. For, though they had always sold their all, their all had now increased – clothing coupons, sweet coupons, food "Points" – so that Caldwell itself was moved to protest. "The World is coming to a pretty fine pass when you can no longer tell whether it's the farmers or the tinkers that are driving round the countryside in brakes."

Sue Tatt had also shared in the rising prosperity, though, strangely enough, not in any material way. It had been sufficient for Sue to feel that she "lived" at last. She began to roll distinguishing abbreviations off her tongue – R.S.M, C.S.M, Q.M.S., Warrant Officer, Sarn't and simply Lance Jack – with an expertise which impressed before if shocked those in Caldwell whose acquaintance with the military within their gates remained long-distance and objective towards anyone under the rank of Lieutenant. Sue had moved from one intense emotional crisis to another with Lofty, Shorty, Nobby, Bootlace, Snudge, retaining her resilience, recovering from their Postings, and even surviving their Overseas Drafts.

There had been an element of competition in those war years which had presented a challenge to Sue Tatt, for, having no fellow-like in Caldwell, Sue had lived in a Crusoe kind of loneliness. But when the

war came, it had revealed that all the surrounding
parishes had, unknowingly, harboured at least one
of Sue's kind; submerged for years, but rising to the
surface, and suffering some great sea change at
Bugle Call.

Sue could still remember the excitement of getting
ready, and making up, with all her little clique, in
this same bathroom, their children skirling in and
out amongst their feet, small nightmares interrupting
large dreams, and silenced only by a sixpence, or
quietened with a curse.

None of the female friendships Sue had made in
those years had lasted, of course. For, although all
were of the pack, each had remained a lone wolf.
Now and again Sue would run into one such crony
from those years, submerged once more into respec-
tability and beyond personal recognition, so that
they would have less to say to each other than utter
strangers, since some kinds of memories shared ever
make for mutual silence.

Oh, but there had been no holding of them in
those years. It was as if all the world had joined hands
and were rushing together towards the end of the
War, and nothing had mattered in between. The
end of the War. The very phrase had conjured up
within itself the magic and escape of some Open
Sesame to a new and different world. But, anticipation, once so keen, had now dissolved itself, though,
for some months after V-Day, Sue had still cast

searching, disappointed eyes over Caldwell, seeking
some kind of transformation, and finding it only as
an exile, after long absence from his country, might
find that the mountains of his memory were but
hills.

Caldwell itself, though, had gradually become
aware of some change in Sue Tatt. She had become
"more choosy" after the War, "more particular" –
or so they said. And small wonder! For whatever else
she had learned from the war years, Sue had learned
comparison. While never being unaware of her own
needs, nor contemptuous of the needs of men, she had
simply discovered that there were ways and means of
supplicating for them. It had been better to lie down
on the windswept target range up at Balwhine, thinking it was for love, than to stand up against Kingorth's byre door, knowing it was simply out of good
nature. Nothing put Sue so clean off now as Caldwell's matter-of-fact approach . . . "Well, Sue. What
about it then?"

There was the exception, though. And, once again,
Sue had created it for herself, in her relationship with
Hugh Riddel; for once deceiving herself only in small
externals, knowing instinctively that any other
woman could have served his purpose, though even
then the relationship for Sue had to become one of
acquisition "Anyone *could* have him. But it is *I*,
Sue Tatt, who has gotten him."

"You stink of stuff, Mam," was all that young

Beel could find to say, when Sue, her elaborate toilette completed, stood once again on the threshold of her kitchen, pausing this time for appreciative acclamation.

"You just stink of stuff."

Coarse, that was what young Beel was! Just like the father of him. Unlike mothers in wedlock, Sue Tatt seldom associated herself with her children at all, but had acquired a rare degree of parental objectivity. Coarse. It always came out.

"That lipstick doesn't look too bad on you, Mam," Fiona conceded. "Can I have it when you're done with it?"

"No. You can *not*." Sue advanced into her kitchen, conflicting roles battling within her – Helen of Troy and Widow Woman Bringing up Young Family. "What you *can* do," she suggested, looking at Fiona as though seeing her for the first time, "is to take that muck off your face, and give that neck of yours a right good scrub. The pores of your skin are going to all clog up for the want of plain soap and water."

"Skip it, Mam," Fiona shrugged, certain in the knowledge that she would fall heir to all the little pots of stuff anyhow, when her mother had got tired of them.

"What do you mean . . . *Skip it*?" Sue demanded ominously. There were moments when her comprehensive methods of rearing her family suddenly back-fired on herself. And this was blowing up into one of those moments. Sue felt an old inexplicable anger falling down over herself and her daughter, and cloaking them in awful proximity. Her eyes took in each detail of Fiona, with the cruel, confining clarity of temper. "Dolling yourself up there in my best shoes! *And* my new bracelet. Eyebrow pencil too. And eyeshadow. You look" – it was either this, or slap the girl until all rage was eased out of herself – "just like a little whore. That's what you look like."

It was true too, Sue assured herself, her eyes still fixed on her daughter's face. But now, the concentrated image was diffusing. Sue turned her attention to the mantelpiece and started rearranging her ornaments. "You can keep the bracelet if you like." Her offer came rough and jerky, acquiring smoothness only in its enlargement. "But those shoes of mine will ruin your feet. I was thinking of taking out another Provident Check. You can have a pair of shoes for yourself off it."

"What about *me*?" Young Beel had sniffed out the favourable drift of his mother's mood. "I'm needing a new pair of trousers."

"I'll get a Provident Check big enough for all of us, then," Sue promised, suddenly feeling capable of bequeathing the moon in gratitude for the lightness within her.

"Got a fag on you, Mam?" Beel was taking every ounce out of the advantageous wind.

"Try my cardigan pocket," Sue acquiesced, equably enough, but you'll have to run down to Davy for fags later on. And you can have the price of a packet for yourself."

"Ta, Mam." Beel's interpretation of the offer equalled his mother's casual bribery. "I'll nip down for them when Hugh Riddel comes!"

The kitchen and its occupants now settled down into an intimacy of a kind which was rarely experienced in more orthodox homes.

"I saw Hugh Riddel this morning," Fiona said, waving her newly acquired bracelet in front of the fire till it reflected its light.

"Oh, did you now? What time would that have been about?" Sue asked, as if the answer didn't concern her.

"I don't right remember what time it was." Fiona felt stubborn. "Early though," she added for safety's sake, her eyes still fixed on the changing lights of her bracelet.

"What time's early?" Sue demanded, irritation creeping into her voice.

"First Bus." Fiona, apprehensive of stretching her mother's patience too far, was yet reluctant to reveal too much, too soon. "He had driven Isa Riddel down to catch it."

"She must have been for the Town the day, then?"

"Must have," Fiona agreed absently.

"*Was* she, or was she *not*?" Sue demanded impatiently. "Surely you know what bus she got on to?".

"The Town bus, of course!"

"Well then! Couldn't you have said that in the first place? How did she look ? Was she all dressed up for the Town?"

"No. The same old usual," Fiona admitted at last.

"An awful-looking frump of a wifie yon," young Beel said, getting the mood of the thing at last.

"Did Hugh Riddel himself seem in good bone?" Sue's interest almost defied discernment.

"Never him! He's a right dour dook yon. But he's coming here the night," Fiona remembered. Her bracelet, reflected by the firelight, glowed like the jewels of story-book memory. "He's definitely coming here the night." Fiona handed her ace to her mother at last. "I'm sure of that. I heard him telling Wylie the Blacksmith that he'd call in by for the bottling lever tonight, because he'd be passing this way anyhow."

"That will just depend on the weather," Sue said irrelevantly and, rising, made her way out to the gate to have a look at the weather.

*   *   *

"It's as bright as day, and as quiet's the grave."

"Aye. It's going to be a right fine night. Mam,"

79

Fiona assured her mother, finding her hand and squeezing it, the only demonstration of affection they ever allowed, or needed between them. "It's going to be a fine night, Mam," Fiona insisted, as they stood looking out on a night that their wish had willed.

You would never have thought that a moon on the wane like this would give such light. But with it was ground frost, and in your mind the promise of the lengthening nights. The quietness over it might well be known to the dead, where every sound was in itself an interruption, and lights snapped up like noise upon the landscape.

"I'd know the Plunger's wife's skirl anywhere." Sue broke their own silence.

"It's all the Darklands' cottar wives making for the Rural," Fiona said.

"So it is," Sue remembered. "God help us. They'll all be singing *And Did Those Feet* and *Land Of Our Birth* the night, then."

"I know. Grown-up women seem terrible gowkit when they're all together," Fiona reflected, as they laughed together in the darkness, adding for good measure, in the great goodwill of their togetherness, "But *you're* never like that, Mam."

"Fiona!" The pressure of Sue's hand indicated the urgency of her question. "The *truth*, now. Say you had never once set eyes on me or on Isa Riddel in all your life, and suddenly you met us both together on the road, which one of us would you say was the bonniest?"

"You, Mam." The answer was unhesitating and sincere. "You are far younger looking and bonnier than Isa Riddel."

*   *   *

On this night too, Isa Riddel, by some mischance or vagary of mood, forsook the local bus and took instead the "Scholars' train" home to Caldwell. On the Scholars' train travelled the youngsters of Caldwell, who were completing their education in the Town.

Not all were promising, though some could simply afford the fees. These wore the colours of the Town's Grammar Schools, elegantly, like casual afterthoughts, slung across their shoulders. The others, conscious that their places in the Secondary Schools were won in contest and held by merit, wore their school colours with little elegance, but with much bravado, as if to say, a thing not worth a damn, but all my own.

Yet each of them and all of them had this in common: Caldwell was home, and sounding ground; the place wherein they exercised their hard-acquired, though never completely mastered, English accents, and gained a genuine – albeit grudging – admiration; the place where they could fall back into Scots, in moods and moments no other tongue could so

convincingly convey, and all without any loss of face
at all.

That once in all their lifetimes when separate
worlds – the town and country – waited with patience, offering them choice of ultimate domicile. In
this, their stateless time, they recognised no fellow-
countrymen. And so it needed an adult without sensitivity, or with the heart of Bruce, to board the
Scholars' train.

Isa Riddel was not without sensitivity. But neither
was the Commercial Traveller, easing himself down
into the seat across from her, without the heart of
Bruce. She could have sworn that he winked to her,
before pulling his hat down over his face and disappearing behind it, though what the joke was, she
didn't rightly know.

She only knew a sense of isolation, as the Scholars'
train pulled itself out of the station, and a growing
feeling of non-existence as it gathered speed and shot
past small suburban stations, ignoring all the waiting travellers in the world not destined for Caldwell
Via Lendrum Junction.

Not even the Mother Tap of Soutar Hill seen from
the new angle of a train eased Isa Riddel's feeling of
outwithness, or lessened her wordless protestation, a
captive there amongst the teenagers of Caldwell, yet
knowing each of them intimately, though not personally. Their new accents rising up all round her,
battling with their old idioms, were enough to make

you laugh, had you not realised its seriousness to themselves.

Her daughter, Helen, used always to be on at her for her persistent use of old out-dated words and phrases. Words like "forfochen" and "blae" – though what others could so well describe in sound body's tiredness and weariness of spirit?

Speech was so important, Helen had always maintained: The first thing to betray you, and the last to stand by you. It had been a long time now, since Helen had bothered to correct her speech. To her own wonder, Isa Riddel admitted to herself that she had missed her daughter's corrections; she knew that one only stopped bothering about something when one had stopped caring about it.

"I know what the Latin words on your blazers mean," she heard herself inform the faces round her. "*Ad Altiora Tendo* – We Aim For Higher Things. Though my Helen once told me that you all say it means 'We'll have a shot at our Highers'. Only in fun, and just amongst yourselves, of course," she added, lest they might take offence. "My Helen took her Highers." Isa Riddel rushed on, afraid of the silence that had fallen over the compartment, but terrified to stop, lest she should fall into it. "That was a while before your times, of course."

The Vet's youngest daughter started to giggle in the corner, his eldest son put his head out of the carriage window and heaved silently.

"I was reading somewhere that they are thinking of making the Highers easier to take, now," the Commercial Traveller said, suddenly appearing from behind his hat. "Your daughter must have taken hers when they really *were* something to take."

"Oh, but she did." Isa Riddel felt that somehow he had the right to know. "Helen got to the University on an Arts Bursary."

"But I thought they all went," the Commercial Traveller said. "You know, with their bolls of meal, their barrels of salt herring, then came out Doctors of Divinity at the end of it all."

"Oh, no." She had a feeling that he was teasing her, but perhaps not. "It was the crofters' sons did that," she assured him seriously. There's a big difference between a cottar's child and a crofter's child. You see" – she realised that he was but a townsman after all – "you see, a crofter works his own little bit of land. A cottar works somebody else's big bit of land."

"I see. So there is a difference then?" The Commercial Traveller sounded as if this was indeed news to him. "And didn't your daughter go to the University then?" he asked.

"Yes, and no." Isa Riddel found herself having to explain, again. "She didn't go for her M.A. And do you know something? I always thought that M.A.'s were what the University was really for. But Helen went to it for a Diploma in Social Science."

"It's the thing now," the Commercial Traveller nodded his approval. "They're all going in for that."

"Still and on," Isa Riddel regarded him doubtfully, "it wasn't the thing *we* had set our hearts on for Helen. Her father was even more put out about it than I was myself. He said at the time Helen would have been as well leaving school at fifteen, putting on one of yon Salvation Army bonnets and selling the *War Cry* down in the pubs by the Docks, if she wanted to put the world to rights as badly as all that. Oh, but mind you, *I* was disappointed about it, too," she added urgently, emphatically, for she hadn't spoken so freely to anyone in years – and the man a complete stranger to her at that. The very realisation brought her to a sudden silence. The wonder was the man was sitting there listening, as if all she said was sensible enough, and even waiting for her to go on.

But that was impossible. Isa Riddel had never – not even for herself – taken the reasons for her disappointment out and looked upon them fair and square. Vast indefinable disappointment was easier to accept than any of its small ridiculous manifestations.

. . . Helen gaining a Scholarship to a Secondary School. Her own rising prestige amongst her neighbour cottar wives. Nothing seemed so worth having from them, and there was nothing else she so needed from them. How well she had masked her pride, on the sunlit Thursday afternoon of that Summer, standing with them all at Ambroggan cross-roads waiting for the grocer's van.

"We see you've gotten Helen home for the summer again, then, Mrs Riddel," Lil, the Bottler, had remarked.

"Aye," she had replied. "Just that." And not one amongst them could ever have accused her of being big on it, in that testing moment. Though, inside herself, she had felt big enough to burst. But "Aye," she said, calmly enough, "Helen's home for a while. Not for long though. She's going up to the University in October."

Credit where credit was due, Isa Riddel had to admit that to herself. Only her own like could have equalled her in understatement. And Lil had done that, right enough. "Oh, is she now?" Lil had replied, as casually as if Helen had just been going up to Soutar Hill to pick blaeberries. "Well, the University will be a fine change for her."

But, even so, Helen's glory had still reflected on her, through the University years, every Thursday at the grocer's van. Once her neighbours realised that it had given her no side at all, their interest became genuinely appreciative; while she herself managed to retain casualness. She could hear herself yet, in reply to Lil's enquiries –

"You're quite right there, Lil. Helen does just look forward to her week-ends at home here. What with all that studying, and all the different classes she's got to attend, and that Town lodgings of hers. For you know yourselves that the feeding's never the thing in the Town. And I can never get round her at all, to take back a bit of oatcake or fresh-baked scone. She says the students she shares with would never eat the like. As far as I can make out, they all seem to live on coffee and tinned beans."

"I never could look at yon things myself," Lil had condoled with her. "The smell of them's enough for me. But never you mind, Mrs Riddel. Helen will be taking her M.A. And one of these days, off you'll be on the head of the road to see her Capped."

And there Isa Riddel's difficulty had lain. How to explain to them all that Helen had no desire in the world for an M.A. It was hard to explain to others something you didn't understand yourself. A Diploma in Social Science just seemed a come-down from an M.A. So Isa Riddel had kept her silence on the subject, and held on to her glory for as long as it lasted.

It was Helen's father who had given words to it all, when she left the University to take up an appointment with a Youth Centre in the Town. Hugh Riddel always did have the release of words.

"Well, Helen! If your Youth Centre is anything like the set-up Charlie Anson has just started here in Caldwell, it's heaven preserve you! There he is yonder, clapping his hands as if he were the Almighty himself. Calling loons he has known from the cradle 'Lads!' Lord, but I can mind when he drove third pair at Ardgour. I was third Cattleman there at the time. And Anson was sent down the road for taking advantage of yon poor silly bitch, Bess Ainslie, that washed the cans in Ardgour's dairy. He never could get a woman, unless she was some poor natural like Bess, with only her body normal in its function. And you needna put that superior face on either, Helen. There's nothing sorer needed than a bonnie, whole man. But yon's not one! Though, there he is, trying to worm his way into the County Council by taking up Voluntary Youth Work. You'd want to throw your porridge up, running into his like first thing in a morning. If *your* Youth folk turn out to be anything like Charlie Anson, it's God help you, lassie."

There never had been a great deal of communication between Helen and her father. There was less after that. Helen had put on the defence of an even deeper reserve. Her man's bitter dislike of Charlie Anson still puzzled Isa Riddel, for Anson aroused no such feelings in herself. On the contrary, he was always civil enough when he stepped across her door. Though what put Anson in her favour above all else was that he was the one person who could take Helen out of herself: for they spoke the same tongue, using the same kind of words. Oh, but Helen always had the best of it in the talking. All the words were really hers; though Charlie Anson would catch them as they fell, and be right and properly grateful for them. "You are right there, Miss Riddel. Quite right. For that is just how I am finding things myself. Only in a small way of course. For I would never compare my own small organisation here with the work you are doing there in the Town. Still, it's expanding. Oh aye, it's expanding. The Minister is beginning to sit up and take notice. But what I really want is to catch the eye of the Rural Council!"

In times like these, Isa Riddel felt almost happy. Getting the tea ready, listening, but never adding a word, to the great talk going on around her. Yet feeling part of it, and quietly convinced that every word being uttered was correct, until Riddel himself came blustering in, confusing them all; for he had a way of sounding right by proving other people to be wrong.

Darkness was beginning to close in on the countryside now. And though officially it was spring, the train rushed through a land that still lay lurking in its winter. For spring was that green something which took the southern places by surprise, but left this northern land unmoved; holding itself in grim reserve for summer's fullness, and autumn's onslaught. And when you were aware of spring at all, it was in some sudden thaw and in your hearing; when hillside burns broke off from mother peaks, and, in an anger of anonymity, roared down to swell the River Ruar, and share its name. So. In this sudden water rush of movement, the land itself would sometimes stir a little, but then sink back – as though even time itself had sounded false alarm, leaving you but the sky to measure seasons. And in the gradual, lengthening light, you would know that it was spring. Such a thaw had not yet broken the winter's fastness. Not even here at Lendrum Junction, where all things happened earlier than in Caldwell.

"Change here for Lendrum."

The porter's cry roused the Commercial Traveller, and set him into the reluctant and contemptuous motions of one who had not yet resigned himself to representing his firm in an area which seemed to include all the "Change here for" Junctions in the world.

Oh, but *there* was a man knew how to face the world, Isa Riddel thought admiringly, as she watched him elbow the Lendrum scholars aside, while he took his suitcase down off the rack, dusted his hat, opened the window and peered out of it, as if querying the porter's claim that this was Lendrum Junction at all.

"It's a nice little place is Lendrum," Isa Riddel assured his back, wondering why she did so. She herself had never set foot in Lendrum, for all her years beside it. And yet she knew that had she ever found herself at the world's end, and met there one from Lendrum, although a stranger, she would acclaim him like some long-lost friend of the heart. For

Lendrum was a sound as familiar to her as far-off Borneo, whose Wild Man threatened all of childhood's misdemeanours.

"Lendrum's just about five miles to the other side of Soutar Hill," she added, realising that this was all she really knew of Lendrum.

"Thanks." The Commercial Traveller smiled quickly towards her and leapt on to the platform. She kept him still within her sight as the train drew out, brushing his hat against his trouser leg, peering from side to side in search of the Way Out. It just showed you. There was a man you could have sworn was certain of his way about the world. Yet there he was, standing lost like in a little place like Lendrum Junction. The image bucked Isa Riddel somewhat. The train speeding under Soutar Hill was making good time. She would home a good hour earlier than Helen.

*   *   *

There was still an hour to go according to the clock in the cafeteria. Helen Riddel sat trying to discover its hands going round. Usually her glances clockwards were furtive, for sometimes she felt that no one on the staff of St Andrew's Young Communal Centre ever watched the clock at all, except herself. There was a feeling of letting down the side about such an attitude to time, in such a vocation. For it *was* a vocation, as even a stranger would have immediately gathered from the conversation rising up from the staff tables.

"We cannot always *like* the teenagers we deal with," Miss Booth, the Warden of the Centre was impressing upon Miss Rennie, the newest recruit to the staff.

A lifetime's acquaintance with her own creed had familiarised it into meaninglessness for Helen Riddel. "I believe in God the Father. Jesus Christ his only begotten son. The Holy Ghost. The Holy Catholic Church. The Communion of Saints. The forgiveness of sins. The resurrection of the body and the life everlasting." So it was small wonder that the words rising up around her in the cafeteria hit her awareness, like drops against a window-pane in a day of unceasing rain.

"But we must always *love* them," the Warden was insisting.

Helen Riddel didn't even need her eyes to observe Miss Rennie's reaction to this edict. Her own remembrance could do that for her – could recall the pondering assimilation, the sudden excited recognition.

"I *see* what you mean, Miss Booth! I think I always realised that myself. But I just never managed to *pin it down* so *exactly*."

Miss Booth was right too. Helen Riddel was in entire agreement with Miss Rennie on this point. But then, Miss Booth always did sound right the first time she expressed a sentiment. It was simply repetition that robbed her words of original force.

"Did you read that article in yesterday's *Telegraph*, Miss Booth?" The conversation was becoming more general now, its topics flung from table to table, the way the teenagers would fling empty orange squash cartons at each other later on. "That article about the Espresso Bar society?"

"I'm afraid not. I never find time to read."

Pride, not apology, sound our confessions. Those bold confessions which defy anybody to think less of you. – "I've got a shocking temper when I'm roused." "I say exactly what I think." "I've got no time at all for sentiment. *Practical* – That's *Me*!" – Those bold confessions; seldom their shabby weak antitheses. For self keeps silence and its secrets still, lending its other images and imitations voice.

"I just happened to glance at the article in the train." – Lack of time for reading, it now transpired, was general, and had assumed a kind of virtue.

"It is simply that they don't *Know*," Mr Fleming of Senior Lads' Group was emphasising to his assistant, "and that is where *we* take over. If we take it from there, Melville. From *zero*."

Mr Fleming had suddenly discovered a new application for an old word, all by himself, and one to his liking. But soon it too would become current: soon it would punctuate all their speeches, just as "Good Show", "Will Do" and "Fantastic" had done.

93

Helen Riddel grinned wryly to herself. How down she used to be on the Doric tongue of her own people! And what a long, long time it had been since she had admitted to herself that they were her own people. And how contemptuous always of the outlandish words and phrases her mother had used! They had become more than balm to her hearing now; they could sound her soul so that it leapt to the recognition of meaning again.

"So you've won home again, Helen?" That was exactly how her mother would greet her tonight – the welcome extended when she had returned as a child from school; one which would remain unchanged, were she to return an old woman from a far country. You "won home" either way: Won . . . Gained. Merited. Attained. On her people's tongue the very sound of the verb "won" implicitly acknowledged all the distractions, hazards and mischances you might well have to overcome, whether on the road home from school in the foolishness of childhood, or on the road across the world in the wisdom of age.

"Good evening, Miss Riddel." Helen Riddel's eyes followed a large expanse of fawn and brown checks, to land on Miss Booth's face beaming on top of them. "This is your week-end off, isn't it? Miss Riddel is fortunate in having her home in the country," Miss Booth turned to explain to the newest recruit. "A country house," she repeated, laughing to emphasise that she was really joking, and having revealed her human potentialities, briskened up into being the Warden of the Centre again. "Let me see, now." Miss Booth shot her arm out in front of her face, pulled it sharply back till her hand almost caught her nose, and studied her wrist-watch before turning an accusing eye towards the cafeteria clock. "Is your clock at the correct time, Mrs Lovat?" she demanded of the cafeteria lady, so importantly that the staff broke off their conversation and turned all their eyes and all their attention upon the cafeteria clock.

"It wasn't right according to the Wireless," the cafeteria lady grumbled. "I went and missed the six o'clock News through that clock." Her tone rejected suggested ownership of it. "And it wasn't *me* that touched it. I've got enough to get through here in an evening, without going and messing about with other folks' clocks."

"Of course it wasn't *you*, Mrs Lovat," Miss Booth hastened to reassure the cafeteria lady. "You wouldn't dream of doing such a thing."

"It could have been one of the lads," Mr Fleming ventured. "They get up to all sorts, trying to wangle an extra ten minutes at table tennis."

"*Robert!*" Miss Booth turned her back on both Mr Fleming and his opinions, and shouted again for the Patrol Boy. "*Robert!* Where *has* Robert got to?" No one moved to search for Robert, but all seemed to be poised at the starting tape. "*Ah! There* you are, Robert," Miss Booth acclaimed him gladly, the way an amateur conjurer might acclaim the rabbit he hadn't really expected inside his hat. "NOW." Miss Booth's enunciation of that simple word adjured all to listen carefully, although Robert, slightly over-whelmed by the prominence in which he found himself, was the one to whom she spoke. "Now Robert. As you well know, I like this Centre efficiently run."

I know it all, Helen Riddel thought wearily, let-ting the rest of Miss Booth's words slip away from her. I could say it for her, word for word; or rather for the benefit of the newest recruit. Indeed it was for the newest recruit's benefit that the Warden was re-peating her edicts to a patrol boy who was familiar with them.

"She's such a personality, isn't she?" The newest recruit sat herself down beside Helen Riddel in a fervour of admiration for the Warden. "She mixes so well. It must be very difficult to get close to that type of teenager, and that's half the battle, Miss Booth assures me. How do *you* manage it, Miss Riddel? I believe you've worked here for quite a time."

"For eight years," Helen Riddel said, "and I've never managed it." It didn't matter now; you could admit to murder when it no longer mattered to you. And you'll never manage it either, Helen Riddel thought, smiling at the shocked blankness of the newest recruit's expression. "You see," she added, kindly enough, "knowing the way and being capable of walking straight along it are two different things. In theory I know the way, and it sounds simple enough. It just means keeping in mind that, in our Welfare State, the only difference between these teenagers and ourselves is that we have lived that little bit longer, and so should have more experience of life."

"Of course you are right, Miss Riddel, you are quite right."

"No." Helen Riddel shook her head. "That's the theory, but it just doesn't always work out like that."

"But we must keep it in mind just the same," the newest recruit insisted.

You're shaping all right, Helen Riddel thought, rising and collecting her registers; you have already got the most essential thing, the team spirit (for she had observed the instinctive natural use of the collective pronoun "we"). Perhaps your face will fit better than mine ever did. My personal distaste for teetering, high-heeled children, rescued from all-night cafés, was cancelled out by the knowledge that even the sluttiest of them had more experience of the basics of life in one wet night than I had in twenty-five years.

She could cope much better now, Helen Riddel realised ironically. But now was too late.

*　　　*　　　*

The bus for Caldwell was already standing in Glebe Street when Helen Riddel took up her place at the end of the queue, though this by no means signified its departure on time.

"God Almighty, Jean, where are you off to now?" Beel Grieve, the crofter, grumbled after the disappearing figure of the conductress. "When that red-headed one's on the conducting," he informed the rest of the queue, "she's just like a hen on a hot girdle."

"She's a lot more obliging than the wee dark creature that was on the conducting before her," the Joiner's wife defended. "There's nothing Jean won't bring you back from the Town, if you ask her nice like. And she's away the now for rings for poor Bert Wheeler's pigeons.

"Is yon mannie taken to rearing pigeons, then?" Beel Grieve's irritation was momentarily overcome by his contemplation. "He was awful set on ferrets at the back end of the year."

"He's on the pigeons now then," the Joiner's wife snapped, turning her attention on the bus driver, who was struggling to put a crate of day-old chicks up on the rack. "Turn that box over on its other side, Davie," she advised him. "You'll have the chickens standing on their heads that way. What are they, anyhow, day-olds?"

"God knows what they are," the driver grumbled, pausing to examine the label on the crate. "Day-old pullets for Balwhine."

98

"You would think," the Joiner's wife reflected, "that Balwhine would just set a clocking hen and let her do the rest of it for him; for she's a lot better at it than all yon scuttering about with oil stoves."

"There's not a sign of that conductress quean coming back yet." Beel Grieve was becoming irritable again. "And I've got a Union Meeting in Caldwell the night at eight o'clock."

"Jean will be holding on for the Late Final Editions," the driver explained, "and the lassie canna get them till they come out."

"But I tell you, Davie, I've got a Meeting at eight o'clock," Beel Grieve insisted again.

"Excuse me," a voice behind him interrupted, "but I understood that this bus was scheduled to leave Glebe Street at seven o'clock."

"You understood right, Mistress." The driver surveyed the newcomer severely. "But this bus takes fits and starts. It's the last bus to Caldwell the night. And I'm not budging an inch from here till my regulars turn up."

"But don't you realise," the woman protested, "I am due to judge a Competition in Caldwell at eight o'clock."

"Good God!" – the Joiner's wife nudged Beel Grieve – "that must be the Marmalade Competition wifie. It serves them all right, too, if she never turns up," she added resentfully, "for they say she's a first cousin of the Dominie's wife; and she's got a good sweep of her, when you take a right look. We should always have complete outsiders to judge our competitions. It's a lot fairer that way."

"Rob Finney's pulled a muscle and will be out of the Cup Final the morn," the conductress shouted from the other side of the street, a bundle of Late Finals slung in one hand, and her own free copy waving in the other. "That's the Town's chances of the Northern League up in the air. And your coupon gone for a Burton, Davie. Look see." She thrust the paper under the driver's nose, and they relayed the headlines together. "Voodoo Hits The Dons. What Price Pittodrie Tomorrow?"

"Dundee United will just murder them the morn, then," the driver prophesied, handing the paper back to Jean. "And that reminds me. Did you call in by Bruntslands to collect yon wrench for Wylie the blacksmith. He says Hugh Riddel will lay hands on him if it doesn't turn up this week."

"God, Davie," the conductress gaped, crestfallen. "I clean forgot all about that wrench. But it won't take me two minutes to nip back to Bruntslands for it."

"You may just as well all get inside the bus, then," the driver advised, as the conductress shot off out of view again, "and get yourselves settled down in comfort till Jean gets back."

"But it isn't good enough," the Marmalade Com-

petition lady protested, struggling through the queue,
and making her way first into the bus, as if this was
but her natural right.

"It's *my* bus, Mistress," the driver reminded her.

"It isn't good enough," she repeated. "I haven't
got all the time in the world."

"But Caldwell has," Helen Riddel thought
smilingly, before putting on the white, serious mask
of Miss Riddel again, and getting into the bus.

"It's you, is't then, Miss Riddel?" The Joiner's
wife swung round in her seat. "I didna notice you in
the queue."

"I was at the back of it."

"Excuse me," the Marmalade Competition lady
hovered above Helen Riddel. "Do you mind if I
share this seat with you? I usually prefer a back seat,
but there's a crate of chickens in the rack above my
head."

"And a great pity they didna file on her hat," the
Joiner's wife whispered, as the Marmalade Competition lady struggled to put her belongings up on
the rack before easing herself down beside Helen
Riddel.

"Ridiculous things, these country buses," she confided, when she got settled. "And, do you know,
although my work takes me all over the countryside
– Domestic Science, you know – this bus is just about
the last word."

Helen Riddel turned her face aside to the window.

She didn't want to be involved in conversation. She wanted to be left to herself, and to her own thoughts.

"Miss Riddel? I thought it was you, hiding yourself away in the corner there." The Vet's wife was now leaning over the Marmalade Competition lady's knees. "I was speaking about you just the other day, with Mr Anson. We both thought it would be an excellent idea if we could persuade you to give a talk to our Churchwomen's Guild on Present-Day Teenagers and Their Needs."

"So you got the wrench then, Jean?" The driver popped his head through the small window, and to her gratitude prevented Helen Riddel from committing herself. "Right then. So we're all set, are we?" the driver asked, his foot on the accelerator.

"No, Davie. Good God, not yet." The conductress stopped him. "Donald Craig's just on his road here for the bus. I got a glimpse of him making his way down the Kirkgate."

"It's just not good enough," the Marmalade Competition lady protested again.

*　　　*　　　*

"Pitmedden Lodge. Stott's Smiddy. Hill of Inish. Tyrebagger Corner." The conductress did not indicate a route, but pin-pointed a whole countryside. No bus in all the world was so uncomfortably personal in its function. "Kingorth Crossroads! That's your stop, Donald. Donald's stop," she shouted, rapping on the driver's window.

"But I'm not wanting off here, Jean," Donald Craig observed, equably enough. "You might just put me down a bittie further on, at Geordie Scobie's place."

"But this is your stop, Donald." The conductress was inexorable. "You bide at Kingorth Crossroads."

"I bide at Kingorth, lassie." Donald's equanimity was beginning to desert him. "I was born at Kingorth, and like as not I'll die there. But for all that, I just want to be put down at Geordie Scobie's place the night. Is there any law against that? Tell me."

"Further on, Davie. Geordie Scobie's place." The conductress rapped on the driver's window before casting a beseeching glance towards her passengers, which implied that any man who refused to be set down on the doorstep of his own home must be clean out of his mind.

"Lendrum Village." No London conductor could have announced "Trafalgar Square" with more aplomb, nor could his bus have entered it with such an anticipation of Occasion.

"Well, we may as well get out and stretch our legs for a bit," Beel Grieve suggested, making his way out of the bus as the conductress disappeared to deliver the Late Finals to the shop, while the driver followed her, laden with personal errands he had undertaken to deliver from the Town.

"This is one place my work has never taken me to." The Marmalade Competition lady leaned across Helen Riddel to peer out of the window.

"You havena missed very much then," the Joiner's wife assured her. "For it's a dead and alive hole of a place, is Lendrum. That's so, isn't it, Miss Riddel?"

"I couldn't say." Helen Riddel kept her face averted and her eyes fixed on the darkness.

Edinburgh. Glasgow. Aberdeen. Dundee. How small Scotland sounded, summed up by its four main cities, but what a width of world its little villages stravaiged.

"I've always just passed through Lendrum in the bus," Helen Riddel explained, "so I've never really seen it." But then she recollected to herself:

> *I've never been to Mamble*
> *That lies above the Tame.*
> *So I wonder who's in Mamble . . .*

"What a stramash there was in the sawmill in Lendrum the night," the conductress burst into the bus, brimful of the news garnered from the shop. "It appears Robb's got one of thae misplaced Hungarians working for him at the sawmill; and the night, when the men were getting their wages, two women turned up and claimed the Hungarian and his wages. They both said they were his wife."

"Lord. *That* had put Robb the Sawmill in a right lather," Beel Grieve said, "for Robb was aye awful feared of women folk."

"Poor Robb just didna know what to do about it," the conductress agreed. "According to Bell in the shop, he just did nothing. Nor did the Hungarian. It was the two women that fought it out amongst themselves."

"None of the local women, surely, Jean?" the Vet's wife demanded, aghast.

"No. Of course not!" The conductress felt contemptuous of such stupidity. "Just two Town women. Apparently the Hungarian goes off to the Town and gets mixed up with the women every other weekend."

"And Robb the Sawmill would *not* have approved of that," the Vet's wife concluded decisively.

"Robb wasna muckle concerned over that part of it, one way or the other," the conductress contradicted aloofly, as one in first possession of all the facts. "It seems the Hungarian's willing and a worker; and Robb doesna want to lose him. So long as he keeps the women from the Town from popping up and creating at the sawmill!"

*　　　　*　　　　*

"Next Stop, Caldwell," the conductress announced, in the wearied tone of one who, having more than fulfilled her duties to her fellow-men, has tired of the species at last; and slumping herself down into the seat vacated by Donald Craig, kicked off her shoes, took a Late Final out of one pocket, an apple out of the other, and withdrew herself.

"And George, of course," the Vet's wife began to inform loudly, "is always the same. I *was* annoyed when the Garage said they couldn't possibly have the car overhauled by Monday."

"We know fine she's got a car," the Joiner's wife turned round to whisper, "so she needn't go on about it like that. We know fine she doesn't usually go by bus like other seven-day folk."

"But George simply refused to let me have the brake," the Vet's wife went on, "although I told him I had to take the chair up in the School Hall tonight."

"Michty! We forgot all about George's brake." The Joiner's wife swung confidentially round in her seat again. "Aye, aye. Of course George has got a brake. *Two* cars. Well, well! We really have got it right this time!"

The bus was skirting round beneath Soutar Hill. Caldwell, spread out before it, was anonymous to all except its own, who could interpret its far-flung flickering lights.

"What's the School Hall all lit up for?" the Joiner's wife demanded suddenly, in the incredulous tone of one who had neither been consulted nor informed.

"God, I forgot." For she had now remembered. "Charlie Anson is holding what he calls an Open Night, up yonder at his Youth Club. But of course you'll know all about that, Miss Riddel?"

For an instant Helen Riddel was not quite sure whether she had been stung into replying aloud.

"Yes. Of course. I know all about that. But do you know something else? I'm going to marry Charlie Anson. I'm going to accept when he proposes tonight."

She couldn't have spoken aloud though. The Joiner's wife was now peering out of the window at the other side of the bus, debating over what was going on up in the Church Hall. It was her inner intention, Helen Riddel realised, that had sounded loud to her own ears, so that she herself could no longer ignore it.

I'm going to say Yes, she reassured herself. I only wish I had said it long ago, when there was no compulsion on me to do so; before my instincts revealed themselves and shocked me. Not so much for what I did, but for the way I did it. No, not even for that. Just that Charlie Anson or any man at all should discover my need in the moment I was discovering it for myself. I didn't know I was like that till then.

"*Well!* That just about takes the cake." The Joiner's wife demanded their attention again. "I did hear tell that Jeems Leslie stood with his hands under his hens' dowps just waiting for their eggs to drop into them, but I never did hear tell that he stood in his parks watching for his corn to appear, the minute it was sown. For I'll swear that's Jeems. There, see! Down in his nether park yonder. He aye did claim he could see in the dark."

And you could, Helen Riddel knew, staring out of the window. Form and shape had loomed up into their own, with trees but images of themselves carved out in wood, and Soutar Hill more mountainous than in memory, so that were I but child or stranger I could be guided by the hand and so exhorted "See afar, Mount Everest rise. See it tilt to strike the skies!" Even thinking otherwise, I would believe.

On nights like this a man could stand stride-legged between the furrows he himself had ploughed, and yet feel alien. On nights like this you could defy yourself, your small mortality, your monstrous isolation. And meeting one of your own like, lie down together in a nakedness of need. Thinking that darkness hid you from yourselves and from each other; and hoping it might turn out to be the perpetual night of all the world. And half believing that should the daylight ever dawn again, the memory of what you did would fade with darkness.

"One flesh." How exact that was. The fusion of bodies. So that I can never tell whether it's you caressing me, or I you. Nor does it matter. Nor do I care. One flesh. What does matter is my own knowing that the flesh could have belonged to any man.

Her father would be beyond himself when he knew. But, at this moment, Helen Riddel felt all the thoughts with which to combat his contempt rise up within her.

It was easier for her father and his like. For all the male in him got out, gleamed in his leggings and glinted on the hairs of his hands; strode in his walk, and snapped in his voice. It was inside of him and it was outside of him.

But it was only inside herself. Sometimes, when she caught her father looking at her, she could feel him wonder how a man such as himself ever came to father such a daughter, though, had her outward looks but half the colour of her inner feelings, she could have had a choice of men.

As it was, she had been grateful enough for Charlie Anson. A woman could create her own image of a man, but first she had to find him. And she had found him. Never the "bonnie whole man" her father was always on about. But was there anyone at all bonnie and whole? Was anyone at all completely so?

Maybe, maybe if one was not begotten, but fell out of the sky, a second old, to land on Soutar Hill maybe. Maybe then one might grow up—bonnie and whole, knowing the fundamentals as time went by: hunger and thirst and cold the way the sheep now wintering up on Soutar Hill might come to know them. And loneliness surely! For, though the sheep seek solitude only in the oncoming intuition of birth and death, their bleating through the darkness would make of the world a waste, and of Soutar Hill, a mountain not removed, yet wholly lost.

*   *   *

James Aiken, the Minister of Caldwell, was approaching Ambroggan Croft with some misgiving. Crofts always did have this effect on him—"the first and last adventures of the land". And since risk lies at the heart of all adventure, this was undoubtedly true of the crofts. He remembered the parish of his Induction of forty years ago: a West Island parish, consisting solely of crofting townships, bold whitewashed houses, their windows searching the ocean, like their inhabitants, with an eye always on the sea; being dependent on both the land and the fishing had rendered them curiously independent of either. Nor were their crofts ever crowded out, diminished or put to shame by large, contrasting farms, unlike Caldwell, whose crofts forced themselves up out of the earth in small defiant protest.

The Minister always felt at a disadvantage in a crofter's house, and always vaguely resentful of the man who could put him in such an uncomfortable position. A farm-worker was an easier proposition. "Well, Beel," he could say with easy familiarity, "I see that the weather kept up till you got in the harvest." And to his wife, "Just a cup of tea, then, Mrs

Petrie, thank you. No! Not a thing to eat, though I must say that the look of your scones tempts me sorely." For it was the tenant farmers' privilege to bestow supper upon him; a privilege shared by the Misses Lennox, and like ladies of small independent means and large Good Works. Dinner was the prerogative of the gentlemen farmers, the Doctor, and the Vet, and his approach to them all – "The ninety and nine that safely lay in the shelter of the fold", albeit in separate pens – was graded accordingly. But there was no grading of the crofter, no easy overtures, since the crofters were dependent not only on the weather, but on the help of their fellow-crofters to take in the harvest, and no light refusal. "You'll just pull your chair in about then, Reverend, and take a bite with us," with all the complete assumption of the landowner.

In all his years of rural Ministry, the Reverend James Aiken had never quite comprehended how thirty acres of land could compensate a man for such a slavery. Unless, unless it was just that – the freedom of equality that the croft bequeathed. Sometimes, though, he thought he had caught the reflection of his own question in the momentarily unguarded eyes of the crofter's wife; but her guard would slip down again, and answer, when it came, was echo: "Yes. Just you sit yourself down, Mr Aiken, and I'll be with you the minute I've taken this mash over to the cow."

The crofts in Caldwell sometimes troubled the Minister's spirit, but Ambroggan Croft always offended his mind. It had lost the dignity of and claim to the title of croft, with the death of Charlie Anson's parents. Even the two or three lean stirks scratching their flanks against the rotting paling posts were not his own, for his grazing was now let out to more enterprising crofters. The wooden water-butt, long since unnecessary, still stood dark and stagnant outside his porch door, side by side with a discarded butter churn; forgetful now of its original purpose, it stood in abject hit-or-miss capacity under the overflow of the water-butt.

"Step inside, Mr Aiken. I wasn't expecting you, but it's a real pleasure. Just you step this way, now."

The Minister's resentment increased. He suddenly felt that he was no longer paying a call out of his own volition, but was being drawn inside the house by some grinning suction.

"I've just put the kettle on. A man on his own, you know, it's always the brew. Always the brew. You'll drink a cup of tea, Mr Aiken?"

The Minister raised his hand to emphasise his refusal, but felt his vocal cords refuse to co-ordinate with his movements.

"There's always room for the cuppa, Mr Aiken," Charlie Anson insisted, scurrying round his kitchen, opening all his cupboards at once, and flinging their contents down on the table. The Minister watched with increasing distaste; for Anson had none of the confirmed bachelor's swift bare utility of movement, but all the finickiness and frippery of a woman, without any of her tidiness.

"Apricot jam? Or strawberry jam? Let me see, now." He dived under the sink and scrabbled amongst the contents of a cardboard box. "Ah. Apricot." Holding the jar against the light, he studied it in the manner of Miss Perks, judging preserves at the Summer Show. "Nice," he pronounced, clamping it down on the table. "Just nice. A little walnut cake, Mr Aiken? Or you'll try a little bit of blue cheese, maybe?"

The Minister would not have been surprised if Anson had suddenly offered him "a fingerlength of sherry; and one of these sweet wholemeal biscuits to which you are so partial, Mr Aiken", in the voice of Miss Lennox. But no, he was still urging the blue cheese. "Good stuff. I get it sent out regularly from Coll and MacGillvary, you know."

Coll and MacGillvary. The By Appointment Purveyors to the Royal Family when in residence; and to the professional people of Caldwell the rest of the year round. The Minister felt his gorge rise up inexplicably but definitely.

"It was the Vet recommended them to me." Charlie Anson's hand brushed the crumbs of cheese off the table on to the floor. "Aye." He looked up at the Minister, trying to interpret his silence. "So you're admiring my desk, I see. It's a good bit of work that."

"It looks familiar," the Minister admitted.

"It would at that," Anson agreed. "It's identical to the one Kingorth's got. As a matter of fact I had it made by the same cabinet maker."

The house, like its owner, had taken its shape from others, the Minister realised, and so had lost original design.

"What with the Youth Club and all my Committee Work," Anson explained, "I got to needing somewhere to put all my papers. It's just amazing how they all accumulate."

"Ah. That reminds me." Grateful of the reminder, the Minister straightened himself up. "I'm on my way over to see Mr Gordon of Darklands. He had a word with me the other day. He is most anxious that the farm-workers should be represented on the Rural Council, and I myself share his conviction. Most strongly," he emphasised, to reassure himself. "He is intending to propose his Head Dairyman, Hugh Riddel, for election. He will have to be seconded, though, by a member of the Council outwith the Committee. I was wondering whether you, with all your – " the Minister halted, searching for words.

"You want me to second Hugh Riddel, like?" Charlie Anson himself filled in the blanks for the Minister.

"Yes. I thought perhaps – "

"Just so. Just that." Anson again concluded for him, turning to concentrate on the teapot, and measuring out the tea with the concentration of an alchemist sifting gold.

"He was a great lad, was old Riddel, Hugh's father," Anson observed at last, straightening himself up and planking the teapot on the table. "A great lad. Not that I really knew the man myself. Just what you hear tell, of course. Aye! He's a byword in the parish, old Riddel." He laughed, dismissing the parish. "As it comes, Mr Aiken?" he asked, lifting the teapot.

"As it comes, thank you."

"A rabid Socialist." Anson stirred his tea and gazed beyond the Minister. "Always agitating about one thing or other. Or so they say. But then, of course, as you know fine, Mr Aiken, they say everything hereabouts except their prayers." His joke fell flat on the Minister's ears, but Anson continued: "Aye. And he could take off his dram, too, could old Riddel. They still tell of how he could drink his cronies under the table."

"But about Hugh Riddel himself?" the Minister prompted. "It's with him we are really concerned."

"Aye. Aye, of course. Hugh Riddel. You'll try a slice of the walnut cake, Mr Aiken? Just a corner of it, then. A real chip off the old block is Hugh. But you would have gathered that yourself from his Immortal Memory at the Burns' Supper last week.

Too forthright was the opinion I gathered from some quarters of the parish. Mind you, there's just no pleasing in some folk. Still and on, I thought he went pretty near the bone myself."

A sentiment with which the Minister was in silent agreement. "*He dearly lo'ed the lasses O*" – a permissible statement about the poet; but there was no need at all to detail the form that such loving took. None.

"But then, of course," Charlie Anson was saying, "the speak is that Hugh Riddel has no little experience in that airt himself. Now, Mr Aiken, you'll just let me fill your cup up again."

*   *   *

That was that, Charlie Anson reflected, as he stood watching the Minister's car make its way over to Darklands. With just the right touch too. Planting the seed; but so lightly that the soil itself would not begin to feel it till it had taken root.

It was each man for himself in Caldwell. Nobody was more aware of that than Charlie Anson. Yet it only needed face all round. Friendly to farm-workers; not too familiar, though. They would take instant advantage of that, himself being one of them so short ago, and slap him on the back, as if he were one of themselves again; and him of independent means, with twenty grazing acres rented out, breeding Cairn Terriers, and always the odd bit job of carpentry turning up.

The face he turned to farmers, that was more subtle altogether. A casual word about their crops. An opinion tentatively offered on local affairs and fervently beseeched on world affairs. Charlie Anson had long since discovered that his strength lay in gauging his fellow-men's weaknesses. Sharing the saloon end of the bar with them on market days, and now and then a bawdy story, for nothing bound man to man as close as dirt did.

Not quite accepted yet, though, at their front doors as guest or friend. Still, that would come through time. Oh, but you could be the biggest rogue walking Caldwell, and if 'twas so your Great Grandfather had farmed its acres, *that* would be remembered in your favour, and much of fault forgiven you for it; or if you were a scholar, for nothing won such respect as a hantle of letters behind your name.

There was a third way, though, and Anson was taking the right and canny road in its direction. A foot in here, a foot in there; Secretary of this Committee, Treasurer of that. Unpaid, of course, but zealous. Zealous!

It hadn't been easy. In retrospect, it hadn't been easy. But he would show Caldwell yet. Oh, he would show them all. He had no illusions about the attitude of its Upper Ten towards himself – a bare tolerance, and a shrewd usage. He had even less illusions about the scorn in which its lower orders held him. They never made the slightest attempt to conceal it. Riff

Raff! Always resentful of any of their own kind with the ambition to get on. Resentment being over-loaded though, and aimed at the particular, was something he had managed to dodge by the ready laugh; the pretence of no offence intended, so none taken. But contempt, a more elusive weapon alto-gether, was deadlier, and always accurate: aimed at the whole man, it left no part of him unscathed or undiscovered. And none had more contempt than Hugh Riddel.

The grinning mask of habit dropped from Anson's face. Hugh Riddel would learn yet, the bonnie mannie. For Anson, now as always, tackled his enemies only in their absence. "You'll learn yet that I was at least man enough to take your daughter on the slopes of Soutar Hill. And virgin. And since then, as many times as I've got fingers on my hands. And if she isn't filled by this time, it's not *my* fault." And now, as always, the blow struck by the imagination left him the victor.

Strange thing, he reflected, as he set out to meet Helen Riddel off the bus; given even a small choice, she never would have been that choice. But, given no other, and all things considered, he hadn't done too badly for himself. Not too badly at all. She was educated for one thing. A great thing the education! She would be able to fill in the blanks for him in his Youth work. Behind the scenes though! For Charlie Anson's obsession with women never extended to a recognition of their equality. Under a man always, as nature intended. Remembering all the slights and snubs he had ingratiatingly laughed off from their sex, the only warmth he could ever feel for them was the heat of rising lust.

*　　　*　　　*

Sue Tatt's uncurtained window cast a pool of light across the road, setting her house apart in an instant isolation. That was another of the injustices of life, Charlie Anson thought, as he drove towards it from Ambroggan cross-roads. He knew a farmer – aye, he knew two or three – could draw up at Sue's door in broad daylight, as large as life, with a sack of tatties or new-killed cockerel as offering, and bide within her walls far longer than the civilities required. The neighbours, ever watchful, might speak about it afterwards, but that was all. Though, Lord, if it was *him*, there would be such a speak all round the country; he would get shrift that was short enough. The character of a Coming Man must hold no blemish, but once you had arrived you'd get more scope. All the burdens of responsibility before the pleasures of its privileges. Still!

*　　　*　　　*

"A fine night again, but cold, Sue." Charlie Anson slowed down and drew up at Sue Tatt's gate.

"Did you happen to notice if the last bus from the Town was on time?"

"It was about half an hour late," Sue Tatt answered without turning to look at him.

"It was easy half an hour late," Fiona enlarged on her mother's brevity.

"Late or no, I still seem to have missed it. I don't suppose you noticed if Miss Riddel got off it?" Anson asked.

"*Helen* Riddel" – Sue emphasised the Christian name – "got off the bus and got a lift home in Darklands' milk lorry."

"I've missed her too, then. My bad luck again, Sue?" His question was double-edged. But Sue's reply was single and to the point.

"Your bad luck again, Charlie. I wouldn't," she confided to Fiona, as they watched Anson's car disappear round Ambroggan cross-roads, "let that creature put hands on me. Not for a hundred pounds."

*   *   *

It was from the moment he reached the dairy to supervise the first loading of the milk lorry, that last Friday started to swerve off its course for Hugh Riddel. Darklands himself stood in the small office off the bottling shed, fiddling about with the loading orders.

"There's a double load, a double run the night,

Hugh," he said, looking up from the orders. "But I see you've already noted it down."

"Aye." The real reason for the farmer's rare appearance at this time of night puzzled Hugh Riddel. "You sent the memo in about the extra run yesterday morning," he reminded Darklands.

"Of course. So I did. But there was something else – Oh, aye! About the General Meeting of the Rural Council the night, Hugh – it's off. Only postponed, like. Mr Aiken, the Minister, has just had a word with me about it. Darklands pushed the orders aside and came to the point. "Do you know anybody in Caldwell, Hugh, that would like to cut your throat?"

"There's a two three might like a try," Hugh Riddel admitted, smiling, "though I doubt if they would ever just go that length."

"Not even Charlie Anson? Whiles I think that if the Minister had four feet, he would put them all into it. He asked Anson to second my proposal for your election."

"Anson! But I'd refuse to stand at all with yon mannie as my seconder."

"But that's just it, Hugh. Anson's not going to second you."

"You mean – he refused?"

"Not exactly. He felt – "

"Of course not. Anson never did anything exactly in his life. He never supped the brose for that."

"It's only a matter of time, Hugh," Darklands was

saying. "Dave Morrison, the crofter, Wylie, the blacksmith, either of them will second you. It's just a matter of time."

"Aye. Just that." Hugh Riddel dismissed the subject and reached for the file that held the next week's orders. A matter of time. And time has come.

*   *   *

"You've just missed Helen," Isa Riddel informed him when he reached the house. "Charlie Anson was in by and took her up to see some Do that's on in his Youth Club the night. Oh, and there was a man in the train the night," she gabbled, knowing that anything she said would be wrong, but always hoping to find something that would be right.

"Was there now?" Hugh Riddel spoke without looking at her. "Men are still allowed to travel by train. Or so I understand."

"But this was the Scholars' train," she explained.

"Oh! That's different, then. That would just have been about your mark, wouldn't it?" He looked at his wife now; her hands, without immediate task upon them, fumbled forlornly with the strings of her apron, and he felt his anger increasing. "Had the man gotten one eye then? Or three legs? Or a wooden cock, maybe? What to hell was so special about him?"

"Nothing."

"Nothing be it then. If there was nothing, let's just say nothing."

Isa Riddel watched him go into the scullery and pull his shirt over his head; he slung the towel across his bare shoulders and, turning on the tap, bent over the sink, and stood unaware of the running water. All his attitude and actions that of a man who was isolated within himself. An isolation as complete as her own.

Isa Mavor. Isa Mavor . . . she began, repeating her maiden name to herself. But it made no impact on her recognition. The sound of her own born name never did manage to re-establish her. When that did happen, and it was a rare enough occurrence, it was almost accidental; like the impulse that whiles forced her to let the cows find their own way back to the byre, when May filled Ambroggan Wood with fat clumps of wild primroses; her hands that stuffed them into a jam jar, and set them on the ledge of the porch window, had some ancient surety of touch. Whiles, too, when she took off her stockings, kilted up her skirt, and got down to scrubbing the stone flags of the scullery floor, her bare knees accepting almost eagerly their cold rough pressure, criss-crossed and red and young, in a pattern of some old familiarity. She never saw herself in times like these; but had she found a mirror then, Isa Riddel might for an instant have looked on Isa Mavor.

"Surely to God you've seen a man out of his shirt before!" Hugh Riddel swung into her vision again. "So stop glowering there, and lay out my best shirt."

"You'll not be needing it for the Election, anyway," Isa Riddel surprised herself, "for God Knows' wife was telling me that it's been cancelled."

"That's true enough," Hugh Riddel agreed. "But then I neither proposed myself for election, nor made up my mind to stand for it if I was proposed."

"No?" Isa Riddel's brief question was without satire. She knew it was in her man's nature to reject anything that hinted of patronage. Burns' Suppers were far more in his line, she reflected bitterly, remembering the Press's reaction to his Immortal Memory. "But no doubt it was the free whisky and coarse songs that was bait enough to lure you to the Burns' Supper."

"Well, no. It wasn't now. It wasn't that at all." Hugh Riddel moved towards her, towelling himself dry. "That surprises you, doesn't it? But if I hadn't accepted, Charlie Anson would have jumped at the chance. I thought that Burns would be a lot safer on my tongue that ever he would be on Anson's tongue. For yon's the damnedest apology for a man that ever I cast eyes on. Though yon one's reckoning's coming."

"He's got a clean tongue in his head at least," Isa Riddel defended, knowing she was trapped, and yet unable to resist closing the trap in on herself.

"He's got all that." Hugh Riddel agreed so quietly that his outburst, when it came, was unexpected. "He's the kind of creature whose eyes are

124

never off the little lassies. Nor his hands either, when he gets but half a chance, patting them where they're rounding, father-like. But if a woman, full grown and stark naked, was to offer him herself, then yon's the creature would go flying for his life. The dirt inside him is all bottled up."

"And it comes out of you. You're always there, or thereabout."

Were he to lay hands on Isa Riddel now, he knew that he might kill her. Though that, he also knew, would be self murder.

"*You* have nothing to complain of on that score, for I've got better places for it!"

*   *   *

The anger within Hugh Riddel had broken up, so that by the time he had reached Dave Morrison's croft, it was outwith him, touching him only at points and in particulars.

"Well. What do you think the weather's going to do, Hugh?" the crofter asked him, searching the sky for the answer to his own question. "It's cold enough for a fall of snow," he said when he had found it, "but tight enough for the thaw to burst."

"You could be right," Hugh Riddel agreed. The acknowledgment easing him. "You've just got down from the hill then, Dave?"

"And not a bite on it," the crofter complained. "I'm thinking of moving the ewes down the morn;

125

they're too near their time for a thaw to panic them, or a storm to bury them."

"Unchancy creatures sheep, Dave." The smile glimmered in Hugh Riddel's eyes. "If they're not riving themselves naked on old whin bushes, they're getting blind drunk on the young broom bushes. And if they don't panic in the thaw, they bury themselves in the snow. And if it isn't that, they go falling on their backs and die with their legs in the air, because the creatures haven't got the balance to get themselves up again. What you should have had, Dave," he suggested, his smile sounding in his suggestion, "is just a two three Highland stirks wintering away fine up on Soutar Hill yonder. Apprehensive enough creatures by nature, I'll grant you that. But sober in habit and, most important of all, Dave" – his smile widened into a grin – "with all yon fine bonnie hair happing their eyes, they see damn all to panic for. It must be a good thing whiles, just to be a Highland stirk."

"You can keep your two three Highland stirks. You're welcome to them," the crofter snapped, treating the suggestion with the contempt that Hugh Riddel had deliberately teased out of him.

A true sheep-man, Dave. Just as Hugh Riddel's father had been a true cattleman. Each guarding his own particular knowledge and contemptuous of the other's skill, though never of the man who plied them. When shepherd and cattleman agreed on anything at all, it was but on the elements, and on the aspects of the soil that reared their products.

"If I didn't know Kingorth had been at the spreading the day," the crofter turned his attention to the steam still rising from the newly spread dung on Kingorth's upper park, "I'd swear that they were at the burning of the whins, yonder."

"Aye. The whin burning used to be a great ploy with us as loons, before April went out," Hugh Riddel remembered, minding not so much on the flame-licked dusks of his boyhood, and racing against the wind in an elemental conflict that always ended in a personal battle; nor on the startled moments when bird and boy met face to face in a flutter of fear, nor even on the lie that echoed round the hill till it sounded true – "The Pict's Horse is on Fire! As sure as God."

It was the width of feeling that was over him then, Hugh Riddel most remembered now, when Soutar Hill stood in eternal time, a keep from whose spy-holes he'd looked down on all the world, knowing fine that he could run its length and breadth before his legs gave out, and certain then that the boy he was would grow much greater than the man he had become.

"You'll step in by for a minute, Hugh?" The crofter's invitation broke into his thoughts.

"Thanks. But no, Dave. I've got a thing or two to attend till the night. A bottling lever to collect, for

one thing. And you know what Wylie the Blacksmith is, for another thing; it's just catch him as can
on a Friday night."

"Maybe we'll see you a bit later on, then, down in
the Hotel?" the crofter suggested. "Some of the
Union boys are to be there the night, giving tomorrow's Agenda big licks and short shrift amongst
themselves. They say Charlie Anson is resigning as
Treasurer. But of course he's got bigger fish to fry
now, what with his Youth Club and District Council.
But he'll be there just the same, with yon long lugs
of his flapping on the ground, sniffing out the airt of
public opinion."

"You think so, Dave?"

"I'm certain of it."

"Well. That being so, maybe I will see you later
on in the night at the hotel."

"There was a minute the night, yonder," the
crofter confided to his wife later, "when I thought
that Hugh Riddel must have gotten sime wind of
Charlie Anson and his daughter, Helen."

"I wouldn't be in either of their shoes when he
does get wind of that," his wife commented doucely
enough, but reflectively. For her own passion, though
brief-lived, laboured-out and all but forgotten now,
still made that of any other person intriguing. "The
thing is," she jerked herself out of contemplation,
"the thing is this Hugh Riddel has little room to
condemn his own, for he has shown them but little

128

example. And it's ten to one that he himself was on his road to see Sue Tatt when you ran into him."

*   *   *

"It's Hugh Riddel." Fiona nudged her mother excitedly. "I told you that he was coming here the night. He's walking. That's why he's so late."

"My eyes are in my head, not in my backside," Sue snapped. "And I must say you've taken your time on it," she greeted Hugh Riddel when he reached the gate. "And you," she turned to Fiona again, "can just make yourself scarce. Take a turn down to the cross-roads for my cigarettes, and take young Beel with you."

"There's no need for that the night, Sue," Hugh Riddel interrupted. "I'm not biding. I've got other business on hand the night."

"Surely your business can keep till you've had a drink of tea," Sue protested, beginning to unlatch the gate. "But just you please yourself, of course."

"Are you still wanting cigarettes, then, Mam?" Fiona broke into Hugh Riddel's hesitation. "Because I can easy run down for them."

"There's no need," Hugh Riddel answered, turning to her mother for confirmation. "That is, of course, unless you really want cigarettes."

"I don't want cigarettes." Sue began to lead the way into the house. "To hear you all going on like that, you would think that I had nothing else in my head except cigarettes. I don't care if I never set eyes on another cigarette till my dying day. Now! Does that please you all."

Following in the flare of her protestations, they reached the kitchen wordless. Its sudden cleanness again took Sue by surprise.

"Sit yourself down, then, now that you are here," she urged Hugh Riddel when the possibilities of the situation had struck her. For never before had he seen her isolated from the darkness of the upstairs bedroom. And all at once she was glad and grateful that herself and her house were both so right for this first objective examination.

The Woman Who Would Have Made A Good Wife For Some Lucky Man. The role presented itself as sudden as that, and began to enlarge in Sue's mind. Not only a Good Wife, but A Well Preserved Woman For Her Years into the bargain.

Setting the table, she began to combine the roles, and with all the concentration of a small girl playing a game of Statues, each gesture became a deliberate demand for attention, and each question a secret provocation.

"Cream? Say when?" *Who am I now, then?* "Sugar? Two spoons or three?" *I've got no real name at all.* "Strong? Weak? Or as it comes?" *Unless you look up at me now and bequeath one on me.*

"Just as it comes," Hugh Riddel answered without lifting his gaze from the floor. "And stop hovering, woman! For the love of God sit down on your backside and drink up your tea."

"You haven't even poured out your own tea yet, Mam." Fiona jumped up out of the silence that had fallen on the room. "Sit down, and I'll pour it out for you."

"I'm quite capable of pouring out my own tea, thank you." Sue interpreted both the amusement in Fiona's eyes and the pity in her voice. And it was the pity angered her. It wasn't fair. No two people should ever have such an intimate uncomfortable knowing of each other. It wasn't fair to either of them, though it was the unfairness to herself that struck Sue first.

"What you *can* do," she stood searching her mind for the worst thing to be done, "is to take that white blouse of mine off your back, and give your black neck that's under it a right good scrub."

Half her life, Sue thought resentfully when Fiona had gone, was spent in taking it out of her daughter, and the other half in atoning for that.

Had you at any other time tried to explain to Sue Tatt that, far from dividing her life, this relationship was one which gave it wholeness, she would have rejected you. But not now, not at this particular moment, when she was dimly perceiving that for herself.

I can easily put myself right off him. Her anger transferred itself to Hugh Riddel. And, true enough,

Sue had hitherto always managed to get a man out of her system by concentrating on his worst physical defects. Pot bellies and bad teeth had been godsends to Sue at such times. But not this time. She knew that, absorbing Hugh Riddel with her eyes and remembering him with her body; for he would never have a pot belly – not if he lived to be a hundred.

"Your bonnet," she bent in a pain of pride to lift his bonnet from the floor beside his feet.

"Aye." Accepting the time-honoured symbol of dismissal, he rose awkwardly, taken aback by its suddenness.

"You've got *other* business the night," she reminded him, leading the way to the door.

"Aye," he said again, pausing in the doorway, for some explanation of his other business offered him a more dignified form of exit. "I don't suppose you saw anything of Charlie Anson the night. I'm anxious to have a word with him."

So there was no fault in herself. His explanation vindicated Sue's pride, and the relief of it almost overcame her vanity, though not her curiosity.

"I was wondering when you'd get around to hearing about that little shennanygin," she reflected. "Though it would never have passed my lips first. I've got enough to do to keep my own doorstep clean."

A Woman of Comparative Virtue – a part such as

had never been landed on Sue Tatt before and never would be again, so not to be resisted.

"It's been the speak of Caldwell for weeks," she assured him. "And, as it happens, I did see Charlie Anson the night, but only in the passing. For yon's a one never managed to win round me. I just happen to be that bit particular, even if I havena gotten a college education. What they're all beginning to wonder now," she went on, undeterred by the look that had come over Hugh Riddel's face, "is whether Anson has any intention of marrying Helen or not."

*   *   *

Helen Riddel herself was beginning to wonder.

"Doesn't that beat everything?" was all that Charlie Anson had found to say when she told him that her suspicion of pregnacy had been confirmed.

"Doesn't it just take the cake." As if it were some achievement on his part, but of less importance than the other triumph that was uppermost in his mind.

"The County Youth Organiser has promised to take a look in by at the meeting the night. A great pity," he added regretfully, "just a great pity that I didn't know that in time to put it down in black and white on the Invites. But then, of course, Mollison's a busy man, and couldn't tell till the last minute whether he could fit me in with all his other commitments. Still," he reflected, cheering up, "it's a start. Once you get the interest stirring at the top, it's a start. And at least," he observed, as they slowed down at the School Hall, "the folkies are all beginning to drift in."

They were, although apprehensively enough, seeking each other out and clustering together in small embarrassed groups, for this particular function had not yet received the seal of Caldwell's official approval – that seal which could ensure a packed attendance even when it was only old Ag and Fish, the Hen Wife, lecturing on Rhode Island Reds. But then, of course, her presence was always sanctified by the imposing notice that preceded her. Under the Auspices of the Ministry of Agriculture and Fisheries.

Still, as Anson had observed, they were beginning to drift in, and in numbers small enough for him to assess them and to conclude that, so far, not one amongst them was important enough locally for him to welcome in his official capacity. A vague general acknowledgement of their presence – "So you all managed up then?" – would just have to suffice until worthier words of welcome were warranted.

"And of course," as he confided to Helen Riddel on their way through the hall, "I just cannot make a move till the Vet's wife shows up. She promised to take the Chair for me, though she should have been here by this time," he protested, examining his watch with an anxiety that informed the observant company he was now a man at the mercy of time and beset by its vagaries. "She should have been here long since, to sort out the exhibits of the youngsters' handiwork."

"She might have had to wait for George's brake," Helen Riddel remembered. "She was going on about it in the bus. But I can easily sort out the exhibits for you."

"All properly named, mind, then." Anson accepted her offer dubiously. "And set out in their correct age-group categories. The Vet's wife knows all about them."

"So do I," she reminded him sharply. "At least I know the work of the different age-groups."

The truth of her claim surprised herself. The small raffia calendars were the work of girls, fourteen-year-olds; they always did tackle something the end of which they could see from the beginning. But, she remembered, fingering the small plastic lady-birds that adorned the calendars, only so that they can have all the time in the world to experiment with their final decorations.

The cane waste-paper baskets were the work of boys in the same age-group. Her hands began to recognise the basket they held, as if they had woven it. The fine close-knit start made by the teacher; the tightening tension of a determined effort to follow the start exactly; the gradual slackening off to the widening gaps which marked that midway moment when boy and basket fell out of mood with each other and the end seemed as far away as the beginning; the teacher's even work again, bridging the moment; the last wild spurt to the rim's edge, and the careful finish applied to all conclusions.

The nightdress was the work of a much older member. Old enough to be engaged, Helen Riddel knew, examining its care and detail. The work of some girl who had simply come here to learn to sew. She would be the first to arrive in the Dressmaking group, and the last to fold away her work. She would join in no other activity, so officially she would be defined as a poor Youth Club Member, and described as one who took everything and gave nothing. "But she'll never forget how, as long as she lives," Helen Riddel reflected, smoothing the folds of the nightdress; "though I doubt whether any of the small boys will ever again tackle a waste-paper basket."

"But surely that isn't the important thing."

For a moment she felt as if Mr Fleming, of Senior Lads' Group from her own Centre, had taken her up on her conclusion. But no, it was Anson who had spoken. He had not yet got the rote of it, but she could feel the principle struggling within his comprehension.

"It is only . . ."

"Only incidental to the purpose behind the work." She supplied him with the words he was searching for, and so coveted. That was one thing she could bring to him in marriage, she thought, watching him assimilate her words and tuck them away in his memory. A lifetime of foolproof phrases.

"But it's perfectly true," Anson claimed, "and not to be smiled at" – for the irony had reached her mouth. "Surely you're not trying to make out that there's no real purpose behind the work?"

"Purpose in plenty," she assured him, still smiling. "So much purpose that sometimes I feel it's like the reams and reams of wrapping paper that conceal the smallness of a gift. The giver has to make it look good, for his own sake at least. And purpose, I suppose, is as good a way as any."

"But there's results," Anson protested, beginning to claim them. "Even here, in my own small way, I'm beginning to get them. Just you take a look at this." He lifted a canvas that leant against the table and held it up for her inspection. "Now this is the exhibit that me and the Vet's wife have decided on as the show-piece of the exhibition."

They were painted from memory, Helen Riddel knew, staring at the flowers on the canvas. She knew that suddenly, but just as surely as she knew the origin of the memory. Searching for specimens up in the Free Kirk Wood. Tracing them in dark blue jotters. Pressing them in dark green ones. Suspended between wood and classroom, and concentrating in a dimness with the sunlight flickering in the back of your mind, so that when you wrote "Dog Violet" more carefully than you would ever write again, and closed your jotter, memory itself would ettle to straighten out the crumpled purple petals so that the mind's eye could see again the splash of yellow hidden in the corner of the flower. The painter too had remembered. The flowers on her canvas revealed all that their natural origins had tried to conceal.

"Take a right good look at it, now," Anson urged, "for the girl who did it never painted before in her life, till Dr Finlay's son – the one that's the Art Teacher in the Town – dropped in on us one night, to see how we were getting on, and just as a kind of experiment like, set them all to trying their hands at a painting. Here, as you can see, is the result."

"It deserves," Helen Riddel agreed simply, "to be the show-piece of the exhibition."

"So you cannot deny that I'm getting results, then?" Her humble admission increased Anson's arrogance. "And that, mark you, without any of your Social Science Diplomas or Government Grants either."

It was his arrogance, rather than his slighting allusions to her own qualifications and Centre, that stung her into truth.

"She'll never paint another. Not unless Keith Finlay, or one of his calibre, continues to draw it from her. And that's unlikely – people like him have wider worlds to work in. You see, he didn't discover a potential artist; he created the potentiality. Not that it matters," she added despite herself, and for herself; "if it happens only once, it's enough."

*   *   *

"I'm sorry I'm late. I had an awful job to persuade George to let me have the brake." The Vet's wife's apologies reached them before herself. "Ah, but I see you've had expert help." Bright with acknowledgement, her eyes smiled down on Helen Riddel, and her hands began to rearrange the exhibits.

"I couldn't label them for you." Helen Riddel moved aside to let her take over. "I didn't know their owners. Except *in absentia.*" The phrase came to her suddenly, out of summers and summers ago, when she had rheumatic fever and couldn't come up here to the school on Prize Day to get her medal. But all her disappointment had been atoned for on the day the local paper reported the prize-giving. *Dux Medallist, Helen Riddel. In absentia. In absentia.* Seen in print, the words had added extra to her name. Spoken aloud, they had sounded her somebody special.

The teenagers, crowding round the table now, laid claim to their own work by loud rejections of it. You didn't need to know their names. Their likeness to each other was such that, if you knew one, you knew them all. And certainly they never wanted to know your name, for their curiosity seldom extended to anyone beyond themselves, so that you became but someone odd, old as Methuselah, to be absorbed from top to toe in a glancing instant, and then ejected in a second's cool conclusion. Helen Riddel knew that, now that she was outwith them. For still and only *in absentia* was she endowed.

It was then that she found herself searching their bodies and not their faces, as if her own body, groping out for reassurance, searched for one in like condition. Her very hands could have questioned such a body, her urgency to know was such. Did it feel trapped by its conception, subjected, in anger with itself, and so repulsed?

The chatter round her began to quieten down as Anson mounted the platform to open the meeting. Gripping the back of the seat in front of her, she tried to break the trend of her thoughts by concentrating on his speech. His words ventriloquised but touched her hearing, keeping her eyes fixed on their source. A man and a woman should sleep together completely naked, she thought, staring, so that when next they look upon each other fully clothed, the metamorphosis is so absolute that neither can the imagination distort nor speculation intrude.

The laughter round her was subsiding, and she knew she must have missed the point of some joke.

"Thank you, Ladies and Gentlemen," Anson was saying. "Thank you. But to conclude on a more serious note. Although I would be the very last to claim perfection for the samples of work you have seen here tonight, I would be the very first to claim that if perfection happens only once, it's enough." He raised his hand to acknowledge the appreciative applause. "At the same time," he continued when it had subsided, "at the same time, all that you have seen here tonight is but incidental; but incidental to the real purpose behind the work."

How naked you felt when the mask slipped from your face, leaving your eyes out of focus, your mouth trembling, and yourself wondering where the mechanism which had always controlled them had gone to.

*   *   *

Outside the hall, Helen Riddel waited for the sickness within her to settle down. Only once before had she been so conscious of her body's separate entity. That was in the summer of her rheumatic fever, when she discovered that once she could will herself to accept her pain's severest spasms, the lesser ones seemed respites, but long enough for acquiescent wonder. This is how it feels to be free of pain. Illusory enough to raise false hope. Maybe I'm better now.

Or like the way we used to work it with the wind, she remembered, its sharpness against her face stirring the recollection. When the wind was in our faces, we'd just turn our backs on it and go racing in its own direction.

But now she knew that, were she to live to be a

hundred and feel the first winds of more than seventy springs sharp on her face, never again would they rise from a landscape where every landmark led to some long innocence.

*   *   *

"It all went off very well, I thought." Anson was as full of his own importance on the road back as he had been on the way going. "I got a few points home the night. You could tell by the way Mollison held back at the end and stood yonder asking about this and that. Well, didn't you think so?"

Helen Riddel's lack of response gratified him. He simply put it down to professional jealousy – an interpretation that suited his mood of general triumph. His mind now touched on the particular triumph. He was going to marry her all right. That had always been the intention. In his own time though, and on his own terms; for a lifetime of snubs and slights from her father demanded an eradication as slow and deliberate as their accumulation had been. Not that they ever could be completely eradicated. Anson himself was aware of this. You could overcome one of your own like – that was simply a test of strength; but you could not wipe out your antithesis – that opposite aspect of yourself which had first revealed itself years and years ago. A small enough revelation at the time, but still the embryo of an antipathy that was to grow to its full height.

It was on the day Hugh Riddel had left school. The kind of day the younger boys dreaded, when all the long-breeked scholars who were leaving set about them, sighting them. Whether by accident or design, Anson had been Hugh Riddel's victim; and Riddel's finding had rang out through the Free Kirk Wood. "Anson's got nothing. Charlie Anson's got damn all!" And, although the other young victims had got very little either, their persecutors had simply accepted the fact as but one more proof of their own approaching manhood. But not Hugh Riddel. Never Hugh Riddel. It seemed to Charlie Anson that, ever since, Hugh Riddel had gone on discovering him, had kept on proclaiming that he had got damn all.

But at last, and for all that, he *had* got something – nothing less than Hugh Riddel's daughter.

"Well then, Helen," he remembered, slowing down and drawing the car in to the edge of Soutar Hill, "so that's how things are with you? God, but you must have clicked very easily."

The numbness began to gather on her mind and left her body to its own devices. Surely, to prove its independence, it began to lead the way to the clumps of bracken in search of the hollow to lay itself down in.

"You might be the better of my coat under you," Anson suggested, disconcerted by her waiting body, "the bracken's damp."

"No." She shook her head and, freeing her face

143

from the pressure of his own, lay looking up into the nothingness of the night.

"Come on now, quean. You can do a lot better than this. What ails you?"

His urgency reached her mind from a long way off; but her body, exercising its independence still, responded to the clawing of his hands.

"That's better. That's more like it. We can go the whole hog the night, seeing you're filled."

*   *   *

It was her father's hands were round his throat; her father's voice that rose to blaspheme; his body that took over from her own and set her free. But neither for her, nor for her sake. She stood in envy and in need of every blow her father struck at Anson. Thrusting herself forward she was at last observed by him. But not in possesive anger, nor outraged shame, nor even with the saving grace of sorrow's self, but just with pity. That wondering brand of it, and brief, which casts its glance on the misfortunes of some utter stranger, then passes on.

"You poor bitch. Was *this* the best that you could do for yourself?"

*   *   *

"But she must have seen the brake coming," the Vet's wife was insisting when Hugh Riddel reached the crowd that had gathered at the cross-roads. "She must have seen it, for I saw her clear enough. She just stepped out from the side of Soutar Hill, and walked right in front of me."

"They took her to Ambroggan House, Hugh," Wylie the Blacksmith was saying. "Only because it happens to be the nearest hospital," he insisted. "For I'm sure that it was an accident. I'm sure Helen never saw the brake till it was on her. I'm damned sure of that, Hugh," he urged, thinking it mattered.

*   *   *

Last as usual, God Knows clattered up into the dairy, rattling his milking machines.

"There's no need for you to sound so bloody busy all of a sudden. It's only me that's here. Darklands hasn't arrived yet."

Hugh Riddel's voice snapped through the empty dim-lit dairy, and God Knows shot up like some soundless shadow.

"If your hands had been half as ready at the milking as your tongue's been at the gossiping," Hugh Riddel said when he himself found voice again, "that lot of milk could have been through the cooler, bottled and off with the first load."

"So you've gotten the first load off on the road then, Hugh?" Darklands, as always, entered his own dairy with the courteous curiosity of a visitor who doesn't know the answers, yet asks all the right questions.

"How's Andromeda's yield after calving this time,

Andrew?" He turned his attention to God Knows, who, surprised by the privilege, began to fuss and fluster.

"She's up, Mr Gordon. She's well up on her last calf. Look see," he urged, "just you have a look for yourself."

A dark face within Hugh Riddel watched God Knows tugging and riving to get the lid off his milking machine. Poor fumbling bugger – fear still made his fingers thumbs; and though there was no need at all for it now, it was a fear God Knows had grown too old within to ever outgrow.

"Let me see the damned thing," Hugh Riddel suggested at last. "It's just as I thought," he said when he had unscrewed the top; "it's that machine me and the Plunger got jammed the other day, and hell and all to manipulate since."

"But you were right, Andrew," Darklands agreed when the machine was opened, "you were quite right. She's well up on her last yield. I could near swear she's doubled it."

"Any more news of Helen?" Darklands withheld the question until God Knows had disappeared down into his byre again.

"Not so far," Hugh Riddel said. "They're going to ring through next door when there's any change."

"I've been wondering, Hugh," and because he still wondered, Darklands didn't find the right words easily, "I've been thinking, maybe, that when all this blows by, you might feel the better of a bit change. I've got a brother down in the Mearns yonder, who has been thinking this while back of changing over to dairying. And I know for a fact he wouldn't refuse the chance of a good Head Dairyman."

Hugh Riddel shook his head, refusal reaching him faster than his reasons for it.

"It was Mistress Riddel I was thinking mainly on," Darklands went on as if he hadn't noticed. "They say that this kind of thing hits women folk the hardest. And it could just be that she's feeling a change might help. A fresh start like, Hugh."

Hugh Riddel shook his head again. East or west, north or south, a mile near or a hundred miles away, the only fresh start a farm-worker ever knew was within the space and in the time it took him to get from the old farm to the new. He had long since found that out from the frequent flits of his boyhood. Only when the horse and cart, with themselves and all their worldly gear piled high on top of it, turned out of sight of the farm they were leaving, had his mother stopped worrying whether she had scrubbed the cottar house they had left behind clean enough for the new folk. And it wasn't until they came in sight of the new farm, that she started worrying about the dirt she was sure she would find in the cottar house they were going to take over. But, in between, they had travelled in some high, far-seeing anonymity that liberated them from every place and every person they passed on the road, and bound them all together in a rare happiness with each other. Much as his mother had always grumbled about all the shifts they made from farm to farm, it was only then, with the past behind them and in the hope it would not precede them, that his mother had taken on some strange new quality.

Gay she had been at such times, he remembered, defining her mood. That was how she must have looked before she ever came to be with his father and himself. The glint of her gaiety caught at his remembrance, but it was wonder held him as he began to recognise the face of a girl he had never set eyes on.

"It would be a fresh start for you all," Darklands was urging still, misinterpreting his silence.

"No." Hugh Riddel had found his reason for refusal this time. "There's no such thing as a fresh start. Only the belief in it, somewhere on the road between the old farm and the new."

"But at least you'll speak it over with the mistress," Darklands coaxed. "Do you know something, Hugh?" he confided, thinking it was his own secret, "I never yet fee'd a man to work for me without first trying to win over his wife. It's the only way I know to ensure a contented worker. And if I hadn't given in to your mother, years and years ago, your father would never have stayed on to build up the herd with me. That was a precedent, mind you. But I hadn't

very much option. It was your father smuggled
the two three bantam hens into the farm, but it
was your mother insisted holding on to them, once
she found out that they were there."

And although that was something Hugh Riddel
hadn't known till now, it was a lesser wonder. But
still. . . . "I'll talk it over with the wife," he promised. "I'll speak to her about it tonight."

*　　　　*　　　　*

"Darklands has just been having a word with me."
Now that there was no need of thrust and parry, and
words were no longer weapons, Hugh Riddle used
them awkwardly. "He was thinking that maybe you'd
like a change of district."

Her face averted, Isa Riddel stood by the kitchen
window, her hands plucking at the curtains; and her
silence, as habitual as her attitude, was not to be
misinterpreted.

"Well, what do you think? Will we give the south
a try?"

She shook her head, and it was but the answer he
had expected.

"No," she repeated aloud, and it was her em-
phasis that disturbed him.

"So you've been considering it, then?"

"No."

"You didn't?"

"No."

149

"No?"

"No. No, I didn't consider it."

"So you didn't consider it. But you did think about it, like. Was that the way of it?"

"That was the way of it."

The swiftness of her submission took him unawares and left him at a momentary loss, for the value of her admissions lay only in their extraction.

"What was it made you think of it, then?"

"It was the neighbours suggested a change."

"I see. I might have known that much."

Nothing, he remembered, ever came out of herself, except her protestations, and these were but contradictions of his own opinions.

"And I can well imagine the reasons the neighbours gave you. Were you in agreement with them?"

She shook her head again, truth needing no utterance.

"So you didn't agree. My, but wasn't that a wonder now?"

"Was it?" She spoke before he could invade her silence, though she no longer needed its protection: grief afforded more, since grief demanded you, and forcing you beneath its dark and heavy self prevented thing or person from taking your attention off it. Depriving you of tears, it yet intensified your need of them, and threatening you, it vowed that never more would your eyes light on other than itself, or smile again. And grief had guile. Clasping you closely to it, it lent you voice for everything except itself, so that you could utter still, without once lifting eye or mind from grief's own face.

"They were wrong in one of their reasons." Her small immobility setting up its own defence began to thwart him. "They were wrong if their reason was Sue Tatt!" He flung the name that had never been spoken between them, to sound her silence, and waited for the ripples to rise to the surface.

"It was one of their reasons," she said at last. For it had been. But she had long since come to know that, if by a thousandth chance, they shifted to some parish that had no Sue Tatt, the need of her would still be there. You could take the bull to the Castle door but it would still sniff out the byre. "Though it just wasn't reason enough," she admitted, as if to something far away and unimportant. "Though," she remembered, "they were only trying to be kind."

"Kind, is it?"

The fluttering fragility of her statement impelled its own capture and destruction. She had always tried to protect herself by stating the obvious, under some old illusion that its small surface truths could guard her. To her, it would "turn out a fine day now", when the sun gleamed for an instant in a sky that was overcast for the rest of the day.

"Kind, is it? Oh, but of course, I've noticed their 'kindness' these past days, I've noticed the way they've all been in and out of the house here, clutching

their offerings of oatcakes, and their tastes of jam,
their eyes skinning the road between here and the
dairy to see whether I'm coming or going, and,
thinking the way clear, scuttling inside to see what's
to be seen and hear what's to be heard. The damned
curiosity of them! Is that what you call kindness?"

"It isn't like that," she defended. "It isn't like
that at all."

"Isn't it though? All right, then! All right, I'll tell
you what it *is* like."

She was listening now; he could tell by the sudden
stiffening of her back, for the preliminaries of their
communication mattered only in that they led to its
conclusion, to that moment of giving and receiving –
that instant of fusion when hostility, finding itself
at last, dissolves within itself.

"This is what it was like." He restrained the rush
and flow of his words, for, loving them, he was loathe
to let them go. "It was like that day the Angus bull
gored Betsy Ann the tinker, in the Nether Park. But
you'll mind on yon day fine. Surely you'll mind on't.
For were you not yourself but one of them went
running in and out of Lil's house where they took
her, with your bits of sheets for bandages, and your
pannikins of hot water. Kind folk right enough, from
the tractormen who carried her in, to their wives who
clucked round her. I wasn't there. But I know as
much about Betsy Ann now as them that were
there. And that's but damned little. Though it must

have struck the rest of you as hellish important. What is it that any one of you mind on now, or speak about at all, when you catch sight of Betsy Ann making her way up the road? Damn all! Except that she wears her man's combinations, and that they're coal black. What a comfort it must have been to all the wives to discover that what Betsy Ann had gotten under her skirts was dirtier than their own. And what a consolation to their men folk for finding that out too. A fair enough exchange for all their 'kindness'."

"It wasn't like that." She turned to look on him now, her eyes refusing to be trapped by any particular part of him, such as his hands that grasped the back of the chair till his knuckle bones shone white.

"And it isn't like that now," she repeated, staring at the whole man. "If Betsy Ann had died on the day the bull gored her, not a one would even have noticed what she wore. Not a one would have spoken of it afterwards. All they would remember was just that Betsy Ann had died."

*　　　*　　　*

"I've just heard about Helen," God Knows said when Hugh Riddel caught him up on the road to the dairy.

"I've just heard it myself." Hugh Riddel neither slackened his stride nor made room for God Knows to fall in beside him, so that now as always they walked in single file along the track: though a brave new road had been built for them years ago, the windows of the farmhouse stared down its length and breadth, and so they still preferred this old dark devious route that covered both their comings and their goings.

"There was no need for you to worry about the last loading the night," God Knows protested behind him, "there was no need for that at all. Me and the Plunger would have managed perfectly for once."

"There's nothing I can do the night that won't keep till the morning." Hugh Riddel's matter of factness surprised itself no less than it puzzled God Knows. Though, come to think of it, man, being animal, was subject to the habit of his body from the moment of its possession. Even the foal that died within an hour of being born could in its final death throe still lash out and image for an instant some long-legged lifetime.

They halted now that they had reached the dairy; for though they walked their world from point to point, their eyes upon the ground, they never once went in out of its night without straightening up for that last look in which to prophesy tomorrow's weather.

Time out of mind, God Knows remembered, had he stood just so, with Hugh Riddel's father, in a silence the one had defied the other to break.

"I'm sorry about Helen." God Knows broke it now. "I'm real sorry."

"Aye." Hugh Riddel's acceptance was as brief as

God Knows expected it to be. There were no words for death itself, only for its justification. God Knows stood listening for them now, although he knew their every qualifying adjective by heart – the very old who were "better away from it all"; the very young, "happier out of it"; the middle-aged who rarely died, but when they did were apt to "slip away", taking their secret word "incurable" with them. Even so, they were the kind of words which had to be uttered by the one and heard by the other. You accepted death, but found the reason for it before burying the body.

"Still, when you consider how things were – "

"Just so." God Knows implicitly confirmed Hugh Riddel's reflection. Words which he had heard from the beginning of time, when it was only the brute beasts that died and man was immortal; and, though time in its passing proved that man died too, the words kept their truth: never completed, yet needing no expansion.

It could have been Hugh Riddel's father who had uttered them just now, as so often he had done, when the "sharger", the "runt", the freak calf, had to be put down. Not simply because as cattleman he recognised it could not add to the strain of the herd, but because its own species, recognising that too, would have less mercy.

"Just so," God Knows assured the father, and waited for his son to speak.

"It looks as though Dave the shepherd was right," Hugh Riddel remembered, for the wind that had been threatening to work itself up into a gale all week had succeeded at last. A fresh gale at that. Soutar Hill was beginning to crackle under it already. By this time tomorrow the thaw would have set in, and hill and element would come racing down together to water the world. But hill would win. Its swift escaping burns, tumbling without restraint, would land as always first at Caldwell's feet.

"Dave was quite right," Hugh Riddel conceded as they began to move towards the dairy; "it looks as though he just managed to get yon ewes of his down off Soutar Hill in time."

Also by Jessie Kesson

ANOTHER TIME, ANOTHER PLACE

'Miss Kesson writes beautifully, her strong, delicate prose full of poetry and humour' – *Daily Telegraph*

In 1944 Italian prisoners of war are billeted in a tiny village in the far northeast of Scotland. Janie, who works the land and is married to a farm labourer fifteen years older then herself, is to look after three of them. While her neighbours regard the Italians with a mixture of resentment and indifference, Janie is intrigued by this glimpse of another, more romantic world – with almost inevitable consequences. Much more than a simple love story, *Another Time, Another Place* is also a vibrant portrait of a rural community enveloped by an untamed landscape.

THE WHITE BIRD PASSES

'Completely frank, transparently honest and deeply
moving . . . she can make the printed page alive'
– *Compton MacKenzie*

Jessie Kesson found immediate acclaim and popularity
with *The White Bird Passes*, the story of Janie, a young girl
who grows up in the crowded city backstreets. Her beloved
mother Liza has 'gone to the bad', her father has gone for
good. This is the exuberant, unforgettable portrait of
Janie's childhood, richly peopled by characters who live on
the margins and by the Cruelty Man, the Rent Man and
the orphanage which haunts her dreams. It is the
triumphant, poetic tale of a spirit that poverty cannot
diminish.

WHERE THE APPLE RIPENS

'These are singing stories, rich in landscape, dialect and poetry; Colette, daughter of a happier land, would surely have admired them' – *Alison Fell, New Statesman*

In these shimmering, original stories Jessie Kesson evokes the vulnerability and promise of childhood, and conjures up both the charm and the dourness of the Scottish countryside. With rare understanding she depicts those who haunt the fringes of society – the old, the homeless, the orphaned and the lonely – and captures each in transitional moments of awareness. Combining humour, and pathos, exuberance and honesty, *Where the Apple Ripens* will delight Jessie Kesson's admirers and enthral new readers.